N GRAY

The Perfect Murder

BOOKS

Vinci Books

vinci-books.com

Published by Vinci Books Ltd in 2026

1

The publisher and the author have made every effort to obtain permissions for any third party material used in this book and to comply with copyright law. Any queries in this respect should be brought to the attention of the publisher and any omissions will be corrected in future editions.

A CIP catalogue record for this book is available from the British Library.

Paperback ISBN: 9781036713652

The EU GPSR authorised representative is Logos Europe, 9 rue Nicolas Poussion, 17000 La Rochelle, France

contact@logoseurope.eu

By N Gray

Shifter Days, Vampire Nights & Demons in Between

Twisted

Lady Hawk and Her Mountain Man

Hidden Shifter

Wolf

Wolf Retreat

Night Hunter

The Fixer

Kai

Lee

Flynn

Jude

More from N Gray writing as Natalie Michaels

Steve Campbell Psychological Suspense Thrillers

The Last Girl

The Bone Forest

The White Dahlia

I See You

Death in the City

More from N Gray writing as SD Syns

The Diaries

Red Lace Diaries

www.ngraybooks.com

Chapter One

PAM

Present Day

I STOOD at the foot of the king-size bed I shared with Ethan. It had only been ten years since we bought the bed, but I remembered that day like it was yesterday; it was a beautiful summer morning when we were still happily in love and wanted to spend the rest of our lives together.

A cool breeze moved the white curtains, making me shiver. I watched him sleep. His chest rising and falling as he dreamed peacefully. It was a stark contrast to my emotions; anger, hate, fury, contempt. The list went on.

Ghostly children's laughter echoed around the room as I recalled our three kids sneaking into our bedroom and climbing under the comforter to snuggle with us. Those were the best times of my life—when things were good and my life *was* perfect.

But nothing stayed perfect, no matter how hard I tried.

I could never understand how anyone could hurt the person they loved. How was it possible to go from loving someone so deeply to hating them with every fiber of your being? I understood that now, but it came at a cost to me. A cost that almost ended my life.

My breath hitched as I blinked, a tear slipping down my cheek. My veins heated as I squeezed the hilt of the sharp knife; my hand pained. My chest ached as the love that used to live there had dissolved by betrayal, leaving behind a hole. We used to be so happy together and shared many wonderful memories. I loved him so much and would've done anything for him. Now... there was nothing but an emptiness that could never be replaced or filled no matter what he said or did.

Now... there was only one way... *till death do us part.*

I stared down at him as I considered my options.

Should I stab him in his chest or neck first?

Chapter Two

PAM

Five Days Earlier

MY ALARM CLOCK SOUNDED, but instead of that ear-shattering screech one associated with alarms, it's just the radio playing soothing music. I reached over for Ethan, but his side of the bed was empty and cold, making me wonder how long he'd been up for. I stretched my limbs and climbed out of bed. Pulling on my gown, I checked to see where Ethan was.

The sound of water dripping from the shower-head caught my attention, and I padded barefoot to the bathroom. Water dripped down the frosted glass, and a recently used towel was on the floor. I picked up the towel and hung it up to dry so he could use it again tonight.

The kid's rooms were a mess, but at least they'd made their beds before going downstairs for breakfast.

I traversed down the stairs and smiled as their voices became louder. When I reached the living room, I stopped and enjoyed the moment watching my family interact with each other while sitting around the kitchen counter. Their bowls were empty, glasses half-filled with juice, and Ethan busy preparing the coffee machine. It filled my heart with love and warmth watching my little family, and nothing could take away this perfect moment.

"Morning," I said, grabbing a mug out of the cupboard and holding it out for Ethan.

"Hey, babe," Ethan said, pecking my temple as he filled my mug with coffee.

"You didn't wake me." I reached for his hand, but he'd already moved away to return the glass carafe to the coffeemaker.

"You looked like you needed a few more hours of sleep," he said without glancing my way.

I stared at him, unable to decide whether I should feel offended or let it slide. The kids stared at me as if waiting for me to explode, but I didn't want to argue in front of them. "No, I'm fine, you could've woken me," I said with half a smile. "I like it when we all eat together."

"I know, you just looked so peaceful I didn't want to wake you," Ethan said as he moved around the kitchen fixing lunches for the kids. "I thought I'd help out today," he added without glancing my way. When everything was ready, he grabbed his briefcase and headed for the front door. "Bye, kids," he added. "I'm working late tonight. Don't wait up." He didn't look at me as he said that. He opened the front door and disappeared; the door closing slowly behind him.

I opened my mouth to remind him about our anniversary dinner, but it was futile; he'd already left. I closed my mouth and swallowed the lump in my throat and, after a brief moment, sipped from my mug, savoring the coffee as I composed myself. To be a good wife, I needed to be more understanding. Sometimes that meant stopping myself from voicing my thoughts; I didn't want to make Ethan feel bad about forgetting. He already did so much for me and our family.

Ethan had been working overtime these last couple of weeks for a promotion he had always wanted, and I didn't want to bother him for something as silly as our twentieth anniversary. The sad truth was, we'd been together for so long it felt like just another day; the same day over and over, every year. I didn't want to cling to a day that had been special years ago if I was the only one who thought so. Ethan's promotion would be good for the family, and it allowed us to send Donovan to college next year. So, for me to continue as if it were any other day while Ethan focused on his job was worth it.

"Hey, Mom," Donovan called, bringing me out of my thoughts.

"Yes, hon," I said, smiling thinly, and trying my best to keep the emotions at bay. I needed to be strong for our kids.

"I have practice this afternoon and will get a lift home from Steve." Donavan stood and wiped his mouth clean with a napkin. Donovan looked so much like his father; he was even as tall as Ethan, had the same color brown hair, brown eyes, and charming smile; just like his dad.

"Okay," I said, my chest tightening.

"Michelle and I will get a ride home with Glen." Sara stood, tapping Michelle on the shoulder, forcing her to finish her juice. Our two girls looked more like me; similar heart-shaped faces, sharp features, sandy brown hair, and light brown eyes.

"What about a ride to school?" I asked, feeling hopeful.

"No, we're good. Glen should be outside already." Glen was Sara's boyfriend; he was a good kid. He had manners, was respectful, and hadn't made Sara cry yet, like some of the other boys who mistreated their girlfriends in Sara's class.

"Oh, okay," I said, placing my mug on the counter, and walked with the kids to the front door, wanting to hug each of them, but the older two bolted out of the house. I reached for the youngest, Michelle, hugging her longer than five seconds and she started squirming out of my embrace.

"Bye, Mom, love you," Michelle said, running after Sara.

I waved at the other two children, who were no doubt avoiding their five-second hugs.

The moment the door closed, a sense of dread filled my veins. I glanced up the flight of stairs, the empty living area, and the empty house. A quietness filled the space where I stood and realized how completely alone I was, or how lonely I felt. There were no more diapers to change or bottles to fill. No more waking in the middle of the night to check up on the kids and whether they were still breathing.

I'd been a stay-at-home mom to raise our three kids, but now they were old enough to go out on dates, do their homework on their own, and from next year, one would leave for college.

It was silly to feel this way, yet I couldn't shake it. The empty-nest syndrome was real. I could always go back to work, back into marketing, but who would hire a forty-something-year-old-housewife after almost twenty years of staying at home. I was no longer in the game and might need to attend night class or a seminar to catch up with what's happening in today's marketing world, and I knew a lot had changed based on what Ethan shared about his company and what they were doing each month.

I knew about Facebook, TikTok, and all the other social

media platforms, but I didn't really understand what happened on the sites or how to navigate them. I simply didn't have any interest in it.

I sighed depressingly.

The more I thought about it, the more I chewed on my fingernails. When I ripped the skin on the side of my thumb and tasted blood, I knew I had to fill my time. I couldn't stand around and wish for a life I had already lived. It was a good life, and I had no complaints, but now there was nothing left for me to do. I had to find something to keep me busy or I'd lose my mind.

I finished my coffee and skipped breakfast; my appetite disappeared when the kids left for school.

Chapter Three

PAM

I APPROACHED the automatic sliding doors near the entrance of the building for the gym, but they didn't open. I waved my arms near the sensors, but nothing happened. A man approached, passed me, and the doors opened when he neared. The frown on my face deepened as I chalked it up to the fact that I'd approached the doors from the other side and not because I was invisible, and quickly ran through before the doors closed again.

When I reached the entrance to the gym, I stood in line since there was only one turnstile working and some folks had forgotten their cards and had to give the receptionist their birthdate or some other number allowing them entrance.

One side of the gym had a variety of studios for pilates, yoga and aerobics, and on the other side, it boasted an Olympic-sized swimming pool on the bottom floor with exercise equipment on the top floor.

Once through the turnstile, I headed straight for the

yoga class, passing two other studios and stopped outside my class. As I entered, someone tapped my shoulder.

"Hey stranger," Tom said with smiling blue eyes. His sandy blond hair was short on the sides and neat on top. The shirt he wore strained against his chest and biceps. His naughty grin held secrets I could only imagine. But it was those penetrating deep blue eyes that held me in place, like a deer in headlights.

"Tom…" I said, swallowing hard. "Hey there." I couldn't stop the smile from creeping up my face. My heart thundered in my chest as I tried to keep my focus on his eyes and not on his full, kissable lips. I leaned against the glass door that was now open and fell backwards. Two things happened at the same time; my foot went out to stop me from crashing to the floor, and Tom grabbed my arms, preventing me from hitting the door frame.

A low rumbling chuckle escaped Tom's lips. "Are you okay?" he asked, still holding me.

"Uh," I said as my cheeks heated. "I uhm." With him so close my brain seemed to short-circuit, and I couldn't think properly or string more than two words together. His grip around my arms tightened, holding me firmly in place, and pulling me closer to him. For me to think clearly, I needed to get away from him. I gently pushed against him and stood straight, exhaling, and he let me go. My arms continued burning where he'd touched me, not because he hurt me but because it was him. His large hands seemed to do that to me every time he touched me; whether it was grabbing my elbow as we walked from one exercise equipment to the next, his hand on the small of my back, our hands brushing against each other when he gave me my towel, or his face near mine when he tried motivating me.

Many women desired Tom Westbrook; he was tall,

muscular, in his mid-thirties, boyishly good-looking, with a good head of sandy blond hair, a deep voice, and a smooth talker. He was too smooth, though; he knew the effect he had on women and always said the right things. He understood his magnetism and used it to his advantage. I understood this about him, yet I drank the attention he gave me like it was the last drop of water. I knew I wasn't special at all; I was just like all the other women gawking at him, so him talking to me didn't make me one of a kind.

"Will I see you after class?" he asked.

"Why?" My frown deepened, not understanding what he was referring to.

"You have one more session with me today, remember? You paid for me, so you got all of me." One side of his mouth curved upward. He leaned a meaty arm against the glass wall near my head and peered down at me. "Or, if you want me now all to yourself, I'm sure I can squeeze you in?" He whispered as his eyes penetrated my soul.

A breath caught in my throat. He was so close now I could smell his deodorant and the smell of him; earthy, male, divine.

Oh, gods, I was in trouble. I thought as I stared at Tom's honed body at such close proximity. I'd never flirted with another man before. Ethan had been the only man I'd ever been with. The only man I'd ever kissed. The only man I'd had sex with. Then there was Tom; he was temptation wrapped in a bow, a distraction, but he was so good for my ego. I hadn't felt wanted like this in a really long time. This was a problem. Speaking to a man just to boost my ego was wrong, and although I had done nothing wrong, I still felt guilty.

I glanced over my shoulder as the studio filled with women. It looked like Dana was already there in the front row, but she hadn't seen me to keep me a spot. There wasn't space for me anyway, so I might as well have the last session with Tom and then leave immediately. I had one last hour with him; one glorious hour with a personal trainer as attractive as him.

What could go wrong?

Chapter Four

PAM

SWEAT DRIPPED down my back as I cursed Tom silently for making my last session with him so difficult. I'd been coming to him once a week for four months, and it had never been this strenuous before. Perhaps it was because it was the last session or he just wanted to make me cry out in pain, and I wondered if he was a closet sadist. Today he pushed me to the limit, and it felt as though I was about to break.

"That's it," he said, his hand resting against the small of my back; burning my skin with his touch once again. "Just one more for me. You can do it, Pam, that's it," Tom said, his face beside mine with his hand never leaving my back. I wanted to move so that he'd stop touching me, but at the same time I didn't want him letting go. I had conflicting thoughts; causing confusion.

I lifted the bar above my head, exhaled and slowly brought it back down to the floor. I stayed in that position, legs and back straight, and touched the floor. Being and staying flexible was important to me, but more so once warmed up, and at that moment I was boiling.

"You're looking great, Pam. You've come a long way since starting with me, and I'm incredibly proud of what you've accomplished in such a short time. You're absolutely stunning."

I noted the words he used and slowly stood upright. He stepped closer, his rough hand heating my back through my clothing. My cheeks burned with desire. I shook the dirty thoughts of seeing him naked out of my head. I was *happily* married. I had to remind myself that Tom spoke to all the women like this; I was not special.

"Do you really think so?" I asked, feigning ignorance.

I knew what I'd looked like before joining the gym; I was slightly overweight, with oily skin and hair, and hardly any muscle mass. Now, I glanced at myself in the mirror and stood tall, sucking in my stomach and pushing out my chest; my body lean, skin clear and healthy, reminding me of when I was in my twenties.

"Yes," Tom whispered, moving to stand in front of me, looking down at me with those blue eyes I could drown in. "You've pulled a one-eighty in four months. You're absolutely beautiful. I mean, you were before, but now..." he hesitated, glanced around and dipped his head lower so only I could hear him. "Now you're breathtaking." His dark gaze penetrated me with such intensity I could only describe it as a need; one I shared.

Tom stared at me as if I were the only woman in *his* world. We shared something in that moment, a connection I hadn't felt before, and I knew by the way his eyes twinkled he felt it too. There was something between us as real as the sun outside, and the moon at night.

My eyes narrowed; there was a fleck of green in his cerulean-colored eyes I hadn't noticed before. I was so close to him I could feel his breath on my face. The need to rock onto my tiptoes and kiss him was strong, but… I was married. Not happily married, but I had been faithful for twenty years.

Ethan Nesbo was my high school sweetheart. We married in the year we both turned twenty-two. While he studied, I worked in marketing to help ends meet. Then, when he found his dream job, I quit my job and gave birth to Donovan, and then two years later we had Sara. Just when we thought the baby factory was closed, four years later I gave birth to Michelle. Year after year I was either breastfeeding or making milk bottles, changing diapers or helping with homework. I was always busy with the kids while Ethan was my knight in shining armor and provided for our family.

But lately everything felt different. Ethan was distant, and I didn't know what to do about it.

Ethan worked late almost every night. He was working towards his promotion while I managed the house and assisted the kids where needed. Unfortunately, the kids didn't need me as much as they used to. The kids were growing up, did their own things and only needing me for money or a lift somewhere.

Ethan was neglecting me, emotionally and physically. We barely showered together. We didn't have the late-night chats we used to. He rarely took an interest in me or tried anything romantic. We were roommates. The more I thought about it, I realized I couldn't be angry at him because I wasn't romantic with him either. Perhaps we needed couples therapy or to spend more quality time together. But there was this part of me that wondered if we should even bother. *Had our time come to an end? Had we lost interest? Should we explore avenues separately?*

My mind raced about Ethan and my kids, while transfixed on Tom's smiling eyes. I felt his body heat vibrate against my chest. My craving to be wanted by the man in front of me intensified. These feelings were wrong, but I felt them, making them valid. The possibility of something happening between us was clear. But I was married; these naughty thoughts needed to remain just that; fantasies.

Tom hadn't moved away. His face was still near mine, and his pupils had dilated as he kept his intense glare on me.

I wanted to cower away under his piercing gaze like I always did, but not today. Today I was confident. Today I felt beautiful. Today I wanted more of his attention. And today I wanted to do something I hadn't done in my life. *Ever.*

I rocked onto my toes and kissed Tom. It was just a quick kiss. A peck. That's all it was and just once. I thought it was something Tom wanted, but the look in his eyes sent me crashing to earth. His wide eyes stared down at me, silently judging me, condemning me.

"Oh, gods, I'm so sorry," I mumbled, covering my mouth and shaking my head. "I shouldn't have done that. I don't know what I was thinking," I said, picking up my towel, water bottle, and bag, and hurrying out of the gym, not bothering to look if he was following me. All I cared about was getting out of there before facing anyone who might have seen what I did. I couldn't believe I'd done that and felt awful. Betraying my husband like that would haunt me forever.

Was this infidelity?

I didn't want to lie to Ethan about kissing Tom, but I also didn't know whether I should say anything.

The kiss played on repeat in my mind's eye, and all I could do was shake my head in disappointment. Right now, I wanted to curl up into a little ball and disappear.

Stupid, stupid mistake.

"Hey Pam," Julia said as she entered the gym. Today she tied her blonde hair in a high ponytail with wisps framing her delicate features. Julia was her husband's trophy wife and ensured he spoiled her every chance he got. Today she was wearing the latest Nike yoga gear and sneakers. The wedding ring on her finger glistened under the light as she waved.

"Oh, hey Julia," I said, plastering on a smile.

"You aren't doing yoga today?" she asked, pointing in the direction of the studios.

"No, I-I…" I thumbed over my shoulder. "I already did. I mean I had my private session. Uhm… and now I need to get to an appointment." I lied about the last part.

"Okay. Is Dana there?"

I nodded. "I think she's still in the studio finishing that session," I said; not remembering whether she was, because all I saw was Tom and his eyes and the kiss we shared.

"Okay, great, see you another time then."

"Bye, Julia." I waved over my shoulder as I hurried out of the gym.

I cursed myself all the way to the car. Glancing behind me, I sighed with relief when no-one was following me. I hoped nobody saw what had happened and decided that today was my last day here and I'd join a different gym. Alternatively, I'd walk around my neighborhood for exercise and avoid all personal trainers going forward.

"What have I done?" I mumbled to myself as a rogue

tear rolled down my cheek. My heart thundered in my chest, and although I was hot from my gym session, an icy feeling crept through my veins. The last time I had that feeling was when my father had died.

I opened my car door and fell into the driver's seat as I continued rambling to myself. "You're so stupid. Freaking idiot." I slammed the door closed. For a moment I sat with my head in my hands, shaking my head in disappointment.

I flinched when there was a soft knock on my window and someone staring down at me. Tom stood tall, dark and drool-worthy near my car. His chest heaved up and down as if he'd sprinted to my car and waved. His face flushed as he beckoned me with his finger to climb out of the car.

I exhaled, swallowing the embarrassing lump in my throat and blinking rapidly to dry my eyes. As much as I didn't want to get out of the safety of my car, I had to. I had to apologize and brace myself for hurtful words headed my way.

Once out, I closed the car door and leaned against it with my hands behind my back. I dug my fingers into the door handle until the tips ached. *Pain.* That's what I needed to stop thinking about the man in front of me. Pain to forget about the kiss. Pain to forget him. Instead of not thinking about Tom, that's all I did.

Forcing my eyes closed so that I no longer got lost in his eyes, but instead of seeing nothing, flashes of his naked honed body came before me. His lips on mine. His warm breath caressing my cheeks. My mouth parting as I kissed him again. I dug my fingers harder into the handle until pain shot up my arm.

"I'm sorry about what happened back there," I said quickly, opening my eyes and stared at the ground. "It was a mistake. I shouldn't have—"

Tom's soft lips cut my words short. His tongue pressed against my lips, beckoning me to open. And I gave in, welcoming his tongue. I let go of the door handle and wrapped my arms around his neck, pressing my body against his. His hands found their way around my waist, pulling me closer, and pushed me against the car with his body. His heat and hardness pressed against my core, and I moaned frustratingly as the clothes stopped me from feeling his skin.

Tom gently pulled away, planting one last tender kiss on my lips while cupping my face.

"I'm not sorry," he said seriously. "Do you understand?"

I nodded. "But it's wrong. I'm married."

"Unhappily," he added. "Did it feel good? The kiss?"

"Yes, but it's wrong," I said, pressing my hands against his hard chest, feeling his nipples through his thin shirt. I pressed my mouth to his body and kissed him through his clothing.

"I want to see you again." Tom breathed, his nostrils flaring as he stared down at me with hunger in his eyes. "I need to see you again." He was serious, and I didn't want to move away from him. I wanted more; I wanted him. I wanted to feel his warm skin against mine, his lips on my body, and everything in between.

A car alarm sounded nearby, and I remembered where we were, letting go of him quickly and stepping away. I surveyed the parking lot and was thankful there were only two people nearby. I glanced at him through hooded eyes.

"Fuck, you're going to be the end of me," he growled low and dirty. "You're someone I never thought I'd find. I've tried how many times only to meet you at this trying time. I know you're married but you aren't happy. You haven't been for years. Ethan doesn't make you happy. You know

I'll be able to make you happy in more ways than he ever could."

I hate that I'd shared so much of my life with Tom, but I was glad I did. Otherwise, we never would've reached this point.

A car door opened somewhere, forcing me to step farther away from Tom.

I wanted to cry. What we were doing was wrong. I betrayed Ethan in one of the worst ways imaginable. But... it felt wonderful to be wanted again. Tom made me feel good again; I felt like a desirable woman, and it was fantastic having him touch me again. I couldn't remember the last time Ethan had touched me that way.

I should feel guilty, but I didn't. I should feel bad, but I wanted more.

Through the years I'd lost parts of myself; I'd lost my identity as Ethan's life became more important than mine. Our children had become more important in my life. I'd given up so much for my family; I regretted nothing, but I felt like I'd lost the parts that made me a woman. And now, after I started training four months ago, I'd found my way back to myself and even more so when Tom ignited something within me. I felt alive. I felt free. I wanted to live again.

My kissing Tom wasn't something I'd planned, but it was also something I was glad had happened.

For some strange reason, perhaps to ease the tension, I burst out laughing. I stared at Tom, who was now sitting on the ground and glancing up at me with a sinful smirk, and we laughed together until tears streamed down my face, and then I was crying. The emotional release was unexpected, yet wonderfully freeing. I didn't realize I'd been holding onto so much anxiety and shame and sadness until this moment. And I wanted to thank Tom for allowing me to be without judgment. I crouched, reached for his face, cupped his chiseled jaw, and kissed him.

This time I kissed with intention. I wanted him to feel how much I wanted him, to feel how much I cared, to just feel me. It was a soft kiss, delicate yet needy.

"Meet with me?" he said after I ended the kiss. "I know these days women just want coffee dates first, but when I see you, I'm gonna want more than a coffee. I can't just have coffee and then say bye; it will leave me distraught." He chuckled lightheartedly. "I'd like to get a feel for you outside of the gym so meeting for coffee ain't gonna cut it," he caressed my cheek, "I don't want any limitations or things getting in our way when we flow. It's gonna be a blast that I can promise." He smiled, and the twinkle in his eyes promised something dangerous; something I wasn't sure I wanted yet needed. "Meet me tomorrow and let's see how we vibe together? Say you'll come out with me? We'll go dancing, have some drinks, have some fun, and then maybe we can do other things. Say yes."

I shouldn't. There was too much temptation especially when he said *other things*; I knew what that meant. It was a bad idea meeting up with a young man who guaranteed to lead me astray. I couldn't, even though I wanted to on so many levels. It was too enticing. Doing the things I wanted to with Tom could destroy my marriage with Ethan and I could lose my children. I couldn't afford to lose my family. It wasn't worth it.

I should say *no* and move on with my life; starting anything with this young man would only cause me heartache and possibly relationship trauma. It was wrong wanting this, wanting Tom, and best to avoid him at all costs before anything went further. I had to let him down gently, and it was safer sending him a text message instead of rejecting him now.

"Can I let you know?" I asked, staring at his lips, and I wanted to kiss him again. My body ached to feel his hands; to feel his fingers, to feel his tongue all over my skin. I swallowed hard and pushed my wanton thoughts to the side, but it was futile. I wanted him in the worst possible way; I knew it was only because I felt lonely, because I hadn't been touched or held by a man in such a long time. Physical starvation was real; indulging in no intimacy felt like abuse. I wanted to change all that and I could with Ethan, but our relationship was strained, and here was Tom, he was more than willing to provide that kind of intimacy for me.

"Sure, let me know when you can," he said, kissing me one last time before walking away with his head down. He didn't glance my way as he left; and my heart sank. It already felt as though I'd rejected him and now he was punishing me for doing so. I hoped Tom didn't use the silent treatment like Ethan did to prove his point.

Chapter Five

PAM

THE MOMENT I parked my car in my driveway; the guilt flared to life. I kissed my personal trainer. I couldn't be more cliché than that. "What have you done?" I mumbled to myself, still seated behind the steering wheel. I was weak, not thinking clearly and had given in to temptation. And so easily. Even though it was *only* a kiss, I'd still given myself over to the first man who'd shown me any kind of affection.

It reminded me of that saying; *'Never become so thirsty that you drink from any cup that's presented to you. That's how you get poisoned. Be selective, be smart, be wise.'*

I didn't want to be desperate for a man's attention, but that's how I felt; desperate.

My cellphone chimed, bringing me out of my depressing thoughts. I pulled my cellphone out of my bag, swiped it open and saw the text message from Tom.

"I can't stop thinking about you."

I didn't know what to say or how to say it. Tom was always friendly to me and treated me with respect and kindness. It was obvious Tom had a thing for me, and my cheeks heated. I covered my face with my hands, and a giggle tore from my lips.

I should feel ashamed; instead, I felt happy.

The situation I found myself in wasn't entirely my fault. If Ethan hadn't neglected me, or I him, then perhaps our relationship would've been easier, better, simpler. Ethan worked constantly, and he did so to provide for us. The more I thought about it, the more I sounded like a spoiled housewife for blaming him. I needed to up my game and to make things work better between us and end this thing with Tom before it got out of hand.

Ethan loved me as much as I loved him.

Then why couldn't I stop thinking about Tom?

I couldn't respond to his message now. I had to speak with Ethan—today was our anniversary. With a shaky hand, I dialed Ethan's number, and braced myself to hear his baritone along with the guilt. The words were on the tip of my tongue. I'd tell him I kissed someone and beg for forgiveness.

The more I thought about it, the more my stomach twisted and ached. If I told Ethan about kissing Tom, he'd never trust me again, and I'd lose everything; the house, the kids, and him. It was just a kiss; it meant nothing. Everything would work out between Ethan and me; it had to. But if things didn't work out, all l had to do was find a job and a new home.

The sinking feeling of hopelessness seeped into my bones. No, I couldn't tell Ethan about the kiss. It would destroy my life. *It was only a kiss.*

Stupid woman!

I had to text Tom back and tell him I couldn't make it. I had to break it off before it went any further. Before I did something I'd really regret. I had to make up for my mistake. I didn't know what I'd do, but I had to atone for my sin.

"God help me," I mumbled.

I readied myself to hear Ethan's voice, but it went to his voicemail. "Hi Ethan, it's me," I said as cheerfully as possible. "In case you've forgotten, it's our anniversary today. So, happy anniversary... I know you're working late, but I'll make your favorite dish in case you're hungry when you get home tonight. Love you." My voice broke when I said the last two words and abruptly ended the call before bursting into tears.

Chapter Six

PAM

ETHAN DIDN'T RETURN my call. He didn't message or send me flowers. If I remembered correctly, the last time Ethan had done anything for our anniversary Donovan was ten, which was seven or eight years ago. I couldn't believe it had been so long ago.

My brows furrowed as I sipped on my second glass of wine, sitting alone at the dining table. My plate was half eaten while Ethan's was in the oven for when he arrived home and wanted to eat.

While the kids ate pizza in their respective rooms, I'd eaten alone at the table. The kids had at least wished me a happy anniversary and even hugged me without asking. I'd felt better, but only for a moment.

I wiped my eyes dry. The wine burned my throat as I downed the half-empty glass and refilled it.

A thought crossed my mind. Ethan had bought me a box of chocolates two years ago. I shook my head. No, someone from work had given him the chocolates and didn't like them, so he gave them to me. He didn't buy it on his own. He'd bought nothing, and made no effort, and this year was no different.

When was the last time we were intimate? I thought, counting the months on my fingers, and then counted again. Sixteen months. It had been over a year since he'd touched me.

I didn't know why I even bothered with our anniversary. Ethan hadn't cared last year either. I couldn't be sure when we started drifting apart. We simply continued with our lives, living side by side like roommates. He slept beside me in the same bed but hadn't held me, hadn't touched me, hadn't cuddled me in so long. He would kiss my temple or cheek but never my lips. Never held my hand. Never initiated anything.

Perhaps I was right all this time; he didn't love me. We had fallen out of love with each other; it was as simple as that.

No wonder I'd given in to Tom's kiss so easily today.

I downed the glass of wine and filled it again. My throat stung, my eyes watered as I gripped the table to keep from falling. My thoughts crashed one after the other as the relationship with my husband became a distant memory.

I naively thought that by losing weight, Ethan might find me attractive again and things would go back to the way they were, but I was wrong... so very wrong. It hadn't worked. Ethan had continued to ignore me in bed. It was only in the company of our kids that he gave me any kind of attention by pouring me a cup of coffee in the kitchen or handing me the breadbasket at Sunday dinner. That was the extent of our interaction.

I first thought it was my weight that had put him off; that perhaps my curvy hips and the bit of a *mummy tummy* had repulsed him. That perhaps he had missed my old trimmed and toned body. And that's what I did. I pulled myself together and started caring about myself again, giving him more attention, but by then he had already lost all interest in me. I'd starved myself for nothing; these last few months I'd lived on vegetables, chicken breast, and protein shakes. The yoga classes, personal sessions with a personal trainer, all in the name of losing weight for my husband. And for what? None of it worked. That was my problem; I should've done all that for myself. Not for anyone else.

My thoughts swirled around my personal trainer; Tom. He was a handsome man. My fingers found my lips, and they were wet from the wine. My other hand went between my legs as I recalled kissing Tom in the parking lot. Heat spread to my cheeks and then to the rest of my body as I imagined what it would have felt like if we'd gone further. I wondered what Tom felt like between my legs, on me, inside me.

I flinched when the front door clicked open, almost spilling my wine. My eyes shot open, moving my hand away from the apex of my thighs and glanced up, plastering a smile on my face. I picked up the wine glass with a trembling hand.

Ethan walked through the foyer, dining area and into the kitchen without glancing in my direction.

"Hi Ethan." I pushed the chair back and approached him. "How was your day?" I asked, gripping the kitchen island counter with my free hand.

He arched an eyebrow when he saw me. "It was fine. Sorry, I got your message late, and then I was so busy I didn't have time to respond. And sorry for missing our anniversary dinner. Seems you're enjoying your wine without me," he said with disdain, glancing at the glass in my hand.

Ethan opened the oven door and retrieved his food. "I hope this tastes as good as it smells." His smile looked more like pursed lips as he walked past and sat at the dining table. "I'm glad you didn't wait for me, or you would've starved." He chuckled. "And boy do I know how cranky you get when you don't eat when you have to," he said, shoveling food into his mouth. "Mm, it's surprisingly good. Well done."

I washed my hands and splashed my face with cold water, using two paper towels to pat my face dry, and sat beside him.

"What did you get up to at work?"

Ethan narrowed his eyes. "It's work, Pam; it's what pays the bills around here." He moved the knife in a circular motion. "If I'm not busy at work, we're all out on the streets."

I exhaled audibly. "That's not what I meant, Ethan. I was just making conversation. Never mind, I'm going to bed." I pushed the chair back as hard as I could, scraping the legs against the floor, making a hair-raising sound. "At least I cared enough to remember and wish you a happy anniversary." I slurred my words. "The least you could do is return the favor." I stormed past him.

Ethan caught my wrist before I could get away from him and pulled me down to his eye level. I yelped in pain as my knees collided with the floor.

"I provide for this family," he said through gritted teeth, spit hitting my cheeks. "I'm the one who puts food on the table, a roof over your head, and everything your silly little heart desires. Do not question me ever again." He pushed my hand into my chest, and I almost fell over. Then he continued eating as if nothing had happened.

I gripped the chair next to me, biting my trembling lip. As much as I wanted to, I couldn't hold it in any longer and cried. My pulse thundered in my ears, but all I heard was Ethan's utensils hitting the plate as he ate, and the silent whir of the air-con.

I didn't know why I cared about our anniversary, or was it only because he'd forgotten? He forgot last year too, but I mentioned nothing then. I'd wished him a happy anniversary and only saw him the next morning. It shouldn't be hard for me to understand that our marriage was over and had been for a while.

Perhaps it was my guilty conscience eating at me. Perhaps I wanted to make up for my mistake even though I knew it wasn't necessary. Ethan didn't care anymore and made it known. I was living in denial and in my bubble. I needed to face the facts. We were over.

After a moment, I wiped my eyes and stood. I needed to understand what he wanted so we could move forward either together or separately.

"Ethan?"

He glanced at me, his dark brown eyes uncaring and impatient.

"I don't know when everything started going downhill between us, but it's obvious it has. Do you even care about me? Do you even want me anymore, or should we just divorce and get it over with?"

He sighed, threw his napkin on the table and turned in his chair to face me. "I've been busy at work, Pamela." Another sigh escaped his irritated lips. "Of course I care about you. This is our family. Things are stressful for me, but they should calm down soon. Don't worry your pretty little head about our family." He pointed a finger at my forehead, tapping me once. I hated when he did that and jerked out of his reach. "I'll always take care of you and the kids. And stop worrying about things that aren't even there.

I know you get bored sometimes and your mind makes up stories," he tapped his head. "Why don't you sleep off the wine you downed, and we can talk in the morning?" He turned back to empty the wine in his glass, filled it up and enjoyed another long sip, ignoring me.

"It's not the wine talking, Ethan. It just gave me the courage to ask what I've been feeling for months, even years. When was the last time you even looked at me or touched me? You've been *busy* for a really long time. Work can't be so stressful that your dick doesn't work anymore." I flinched the moment the words flew out, and I cupped my mouth, not believing I had said that to him. I'd said nothing so vulgar before. "I'm sorry," I said quickly, backing away from him. "I didn't mean it."

Ethan flew out of his seat and pushed me. My head hit the wall, sending a dull pain into my skull, as one hand curled around my neck while the other reached between my legs.

"Is this what you want?" he breathed near the shell of my ear. "You're normally so dry here, you should drink wine every day if it makes you so wet and horny for my dick." His fingers found what he was looking for while his other hand squeezed harder, cutting off my air supply.

I gasped in surprise as I clawed at the hand around my neck, but also experienced pleasure. Guilt washed over me again; I should've been afraid but wasn't. We had never explored something so adventurous in bed before, and it surprised me how much I enjoyed it. I relaxed as one hand held onto his wrist near my throat in case he squeezed harder, and the other loosened his belt buckle and unzipped his pants. I pulled him free and stroked his length. He groaned into my neck, making my hair there stand up.

He shoved his fingers deeper into me and then pulled

them out. He licked his fingers and hummed. "At least you still taste good. I'd almost forgotten what it was like." He let go of my neck, spun me around, bent me over the dining table and ripped off my underwear. "For years you never wanted me to touch you. You always made excuses not to have sex with me. It was a headache or whatever excuse you used for the day. But now... now you make out as if it's my fault," he grunted as he readied himself. "Is this what you want?" he whispered hoarsely behind me. He didn't wait for my reply and shoved himself inside, tearing a painful moan from me. He gripped my shoulders, ensuring he had full control over me as he pushed deeper with each stroke. Ethan found his rhythm, his hands hot on my shoulders, and rocked his hips into me, sensually yet with an edge of pain.

I should've felt dirty bent over the dining table with my ass in the air and my husband riding me like he was trying to fuck his problems away. Our kids were still awake upstairs and could come down any second, but we didn't care.

The slapping sound of skin hitting skin sent goosebumps throughout my body. With each hard thrust, pain ripped through me. Perhaps this was what we needed, to expel pent-up frustration on each other. I'd never felt such violence from Ethan before. I wanted to enjoy it, but he kept thrusting harder and harder. It's as if he wanted to teach me a lesson or to show me how much control he had over me.

The mix of sensations was overwhelming, pleasure versus pain, and the combination of emotions swirling inside of me.

Ethan slowed his thrusts. I felt the growing need between my legs and moved my hand between there, rubbing my sensitive nub to push me over the edge. I squeezed around Ethan, and he let loose at the same time. His grip on me eased as he stilled. He fell onto my back and kissed my shoulder. He tried pulling the sleeve of my dress up he'd torn.

"Sorry about that." He patted my shoulder and kissed my neck. He pulled out and zipped up. "I'm going to shower."

I immediately felt the loss of him, and the emptiness swarmed around me again as if what had happened didn't help. Our brief contact didn't bring us closer. I felt far removed from him now more than ever before. I felt used along with something else I couldn't describe and crumpled to the floor in tears. I pulled up the torn sleeve he'd ruined, and I'd gladly throw the dress away; desperately not wanting to remember what had happened ever again.

After a moment, I picked myself and the torn underwear up off the floor. My need for a shower overwhelmed me; I felt dirty and bad, and not in a sexy way. I threw my torn underwear in the trashcan, cleared the table, and wiped the countertops.

Glancing at the mantelpiece, at the photos there including Ethan's sister, guilt washed over me; it's like my family and his had watched us. I shuddered with shame. I wiped down the countertops and table again, and when everything sparkled and the room was as it should be, I felt better.

The shower stopped the moment I entered the bedroom. Ethan exited with a towel around his waist. He fetched underwear out of the drawer and pulled it on, hung up the towel and climbed into bed. He did all that without glancing my way.

I entered the bathroom and removed my torn dress. Turning slowly, my eyes widened when I saw my reflection in the mirror. There were scratches on my back and arm, and it ached between my legs. When I glanced down, I noted some blood, not much, but it was there. He was a little too rough and had hurt me. He'd never been like this before.

I climbed into the shower and cried.

———

I'D THOUGHT I wanted things to get better between Ethan and me, but after what had happened, I wasn't so sure anymore. I needed space now that everything felt strained between us, and decided I'd go out with Tom tomorrow.

It was late and as much as I didn't want to disturb Tom, I wanted to message him. I picked up my phone to respond to his text. "I can't stop thinking about you either. Is this wrong?" I knew it was wrong; I needed to know his opinion.

It didn't take Tom long to respond, making me wonder if he slept with his phone beside him. *"No, absolutely not. Don't think that. We're meant to be together; you'll see when I'm near you; you'll feel it instantly. Trust the process. I'll get you hooked on me in no time :-) I can't wait to see you tomorrow."*

Butterflies swarmed in my stomach as I read his words; they frightened me but also excited me. I looked forward to seeing him tomorrow night.

"Sweet dreams, babes," he messaged without waiting for my response.

"Goodnight. I look forward to tomorrow." I closed my eyes and pressed *Send*, hearing the familiar swish sound as the text was sent.

Chapter Seven

PAM

"HEY, BABE," Ethan said.

I felt his lips against my neck, his arm around my waist, and it felt like old times. I smiled, finding comfort in his embrace. We used to enjoy early morning sex, would eat breakfast and then had another round before showering. That's when we were young, carefree, and before we had kids. I flinched when his hands moved between my legs.

"You see, that's why we don't have sex anymore. You jump every time I touch you." He grumbled and moved away from me. The tone in his voice sent a chill down my spine, as the cold air caressed my naked flesh. He climbed off the bed, leaving me in despair.

"We were rough last night, that's all," I said, sounding desperate. "Give me a day or two, and it will be fine again. Promise. Come back, please. Can we cuddle? You know I love cuddling with you."

"Yeah, whatever." He sulked as he left the bedroom. "I need to get ready. Someone must make money in this house."

I blinked back tears, climbed out of bed, and used the bathroom. I couldn't change his mind, so I wouldn't bother. He was the type of man who stayed angry for long periods of time, his silent treatment the answer for everything. If I didn't agree with something, he'd ignore me. If I wanted to speak to him about something that bothered me; he'd accuse me of starting a fight and then would ignore me. Silence was always his answer.

I pulled on my robe, traversed down the stairs, and found my family in the kitchen.

I felt a difference in the atmosphere that wasn't present yesterday morning; Ethan's quiet, yet angry, manner was so thick I could cut it with a knife. It seemed the children felt his chill too but were smart enough not to mention it.

Donovan, Sara, and Michelle ate silently while Ethan stomped around the kitchen making coffee. He slammed the cupboard door closed after retrieving his mug, followed by slamming the fridge door once he had the milk.

Although the kitchen and dining area were clean, I felt the stain from last night against my skin as if I'd rolled around in mud. I watched my family from a distance, not wanting to leave the grime of the previous night's escapade on them. It was dirty, rough and raw, something we'd never done before, and I wondered if that was what Ethan truly desired; sex so rough that I could barely walk and was in pain. I shuddered at the thought. *Where did he see such things?*

I kissed each child on the cheek and received a half kiss in return, each focused on whatever book they were reading as they avoided their father. When I passed Ethan, he refrained from touching me, poured his coffee and moved away from me to sit beside Sara.

With my back to them, my chin trembled as I reached to grab a mug and filled it with coffee. I swallowed the sad emotions threatening to spill. The back of my throat ached as I bit back tears. I didn't know why I felt the way I did, and tried as hard as possible not to cry in front of them. I'd be strong; more for myself than for them.

After the first sip of coffee, I felt better and finally turned to face them as they finished breakfast, and Ethan stayed engrossed with the newspaper.

"Anything interesting today?" I asked once I trusted my voice not to sound like a wounded animal.

"Nah," he mumbled without glancing in my direction. "Same stories, different day."

"Would you mind passing it to me once you're finished?"

"Uh-huh."

I sat beside Donovan and watched him page through his homework. "Everything up to date? Do you need help with anything?"

"Nope, all good. I have a test today, so I'm just going over everything before I leave," he said.

"Good luck," I said, smiling to no-one.

"How about you two?"

"All good, thanks, Mom." Sara chirped happily, finishing her toast.

"Good," Michelle said as she glanced up with a broad smile. "Can I still sleep over at the Kellan's the weekend?"

"From tonight?"

"Uh-huh."

"Oh, Mom, before I forget, I'm going to Alley—"

"I'll be at Steve's," Donovan interrupted Sara.

"Are all three of you sleeping out for the weekend?"

My kids glanced at me, then at each other and nodded. They said, "Yes" at the same time, too.

"I have a business trip, but I'll be back late tomorrow evening," Ethan said, still reading the paper.

I faced him, but he continued reading the paper.

"Looks like you have the house to yourself," Donovan said playfully, his smile brightening his face. His expression made my heart swell with love. "Don't get into trouble," he teased.

I grabbed Donovan's hand and squeezed. "I won't, *Mom*, I promise," I said in a tone mocking my kids the way they usually spoke to me.

"We've got to go. Bye Mom, bye Dad, love you," Michelle said and stood when Sara did.

"Yeah, me too." Donovan kissed me on the cheek and followed his sisters out the door.

Once the kids were gone, the silence between us became heavy and uncomfortable.

"I enjoyed last night," I said, trying to break the ice.

"Huh," Ethan glanced up. "Oh, yeah, it was okay." He shrugged.

I wasn't sure whether I should say anything to make him feel better but knew I couldn't let him leave on a business trip with things unsaid.

"It's not that I don't want you to touch me—"

"I can't do this now with you." Ethan stood and finished his coffee. "Forget about it; it's nothing." He plastered on the fake smile he used for his clients, which only lasted a second and then went back to his moody facade. "You're going through a thing, I get it. Next time, I'll try not to be completely engrossed in the moment or be so rough with you. Heaven forbid I enjoy myself too much."

"That's not fair, and you know it."

I stood and moved around the island, but Ethan was

already heading towards the front door, reaching for his weekend bag I'd only noticed now.

"I'll call you when I arrive at the hotel."

I hurried to his side, not wanting him to leave me. He'd said things in such a way that I felt hollow and sad. "Another conference?" I pleaded.

"Yeah," he kissed my temple. "I might have a business lunch on Sunday, but I'll let you know if it doesn't pan out, or I'll be back tomorrow. Okay?"

"Okay," I smiled meekly and held the door open for him. "Travel safely." As Ethan descended the stairs, I asked again. "Where are you going?"

He continued walking and said over his shoulder. "Milwaukee."

Chapter Eight

PAM

I WATCHED Dana twist off the cap of her bottle, sipped some water, then sucked on the lid before closing it again. We met each other when I joined yoga class about six months ago. I couldn't remember how our friendship had started. One day we were strangers; then, by the following weekend, we were eating lunch together. Dana was the one who dragged me to yoga class even though I didn't want to go. It was only in these last four months that I attended religiously.

Dana Mulder was a private investigator and had her own business here in Chicago. We were about the same height, and where she had an athletic build, I was more soft and round. Today, her auburn hair was in a high ponytail, opening up her features, and her brown eyes seemed to pop with the makeup she wore. She married a detective named James, who worked with her brother Donnie. I had met none of them, but I felt like I knew them the way she spoke about them.

She'd also cheated death when the man stalking her

received the ending he deserved. Dana was a strong-willed woman who was still compassionate and kind, and continued with her life as if nothing so traumatic had ever happened. And I was grateful to be her friend.

I watched Dana chew her food finished and then carried on with her story. "…and this client slapped her cheating husband, handed me the cash along with a bonus. Her husband begged her for forgiveness, but she went through with the divorce. She's now one of the richest women in the city," she said, grinning.

"How much do you charge?" It never occurred to me to ask her anything about her services, and today I'd rather talk about her than about myself. I wanted to forget last night and the fact that I was alone for the weekend.

"It depends on the type of service they need, how long I take to complete the job, and what they're able to afford. Sometimes I do it for free for someone in desperate need of answers but can't afford it." She licked the sauce from her fingers and then wiped her hands on her napkin. "Although I don't have to work, I enjoy it. I mean, James keeps telling me I can stop working, but," she shrugged, "I enjoy doing something meaningful, you know. Otherwise, what will I do with myself." She glanced at a woman stepping out of the nail salon.

I nodded. "Sure," I said. "It makes sense. There's nothing wrong with being independent."

"You've been awfully quiet today. Is everything okay at home?" She tilted her head to one side as if trying to read my mind; her eyes missed nothing.

"Everything's fine," I said quietly and tried to smile but knew Dana could spot my fake face. She was an investigator; she easily picked up on these things. "The kids are at that age where they don't need me anymore, and Ethan has been very busy lately."

"Hmm, I'll bet." Dana leaned against the chairback and folded her arms. She hadn't met Ethan, but I knew she didn't like him and was kind enough not to tell me all the reasons she thought he wasn't a nice man. "I know you don't want to hear it, but maybe he's seeing someone else." She arched both eyebrows.

I was quiet for a moment, allowing her words to sink in; words I didn't want to hear. Words I refused to entertain, even though I knew it was a possibility. "I don't want to talk about it," I finally said.

"Sticking your head in the sand isn't good for anyone, Pam. And yes," she raised her hand to stop me from interrupting, "I know you know, but maybe you need to stop being your family's doormat and start sticking up for yourself. You're allowed a voice, and to have some fun of your own."

I finished my orange juice and coughed into my hand; sometimes the juice did that. One thing about Dana she always spoke the truth without hurting feelings; I appreciated that in her, and her wanting to protect and uplift me.

"Where were you yesterday? I missed you at yoga," she continued. "And this morning I saw your trainer." She stared at me knowingly.

"I need to tell you something." My cheeks heated, and my core tightened thinking about the kiss I shared with Tom. I could trust Dana, but it still felt awkward sharing this with her, and I felt juvenile speaking about a kiss.

"Oh," Dana sat forward with her elbows on the table and steepled her fingers under her chin. She batted her eyelashes, making me smile. "Tell me everything, or do I have to investigate."

"Haha, no, you don't have to investigate," I said, exhaling a shaky breath. "We kissed." My ears burned and knew my face was beet red.

Dana sat back. "Are you serious?"

"Yes, it was only a kiss. But…" I said nervously. Dana motioned for me to continue. "It's so much more than just a kiss; it's more than physical attraction even though I'm sure if we were somewhere private it would've gone further. The way he spoke to me, looked at me, held me; there's more to it than just a kiss."

"When did this happen?" she asked, her eyes not leaving mine.

"Yesterday morning after my last session with him, and he wants me to go out with him tonight."

"Where?"

"Some club or warehouse in Chicago's industrial area."

"Are you going to go?" she asked with concern in her tone.

"I said yes, but I'm scared. I haven't been out clubbing in years, and I'm there with a man who isn't my husband. I'm nervous." Saying this out loud left me nauseous, and I started chewing on my bottom lip. "Perhaps I should cancel. I dunno now."

"If you want, James and I can join you? We can double-date. That way you won't be alone, and if you feel uncomfortable at any time, we'll be there and can take you home."

My smile reached my eyes. "Okay, that's a wonderful idea. Thank you. That way, I won't feel the pressure of being out on my own."

Chapter Nine

PAM

THE KIDS HAD TEXTED, letting me know they were safe at their friend's houses. Donovan was going to a football game with Steve. Sara and Alley were on their way to the movies; no doubt Glen would be there too. I knew Sara and Glen hadn't done *it* yet, so there was nothing for me to worry about. For now. And Michelle was with Jackie and her family at their cabin by the lake.

Ethan hadn't texted or called even after he'd read my messages. I decided to leave him alone; it was no use forcing the issue when it was clear he didn't want to talk about it or even pay me any attention.

I pulled my dress down, neatening it. I still had some curves, so the dress didn't hang on me, and wondered whether I should rather wear jeans and a blouse. When I reached for my cellphone to ask Dana what she thought, the doorbell chimed.

Dana stood with a broad smile on her face when I opened the door. "What are you smiling about?" I asked, smiling at her.

"You look stunning," she said. "Although I wouldn't wear a dress, this is a club, and you get nasty people who would touch you the way you don't like," she shuddered. "Let's find something just as sexy but not too sexy, if you know what I mean."

Dana handed me a top I considered too risky; one I hadn't worn in years. The black top had thin straps and was made of thin material; one could see the black bra underneath. I grabbed my casual black jacket to wear over it and completed the outfit with jeans and low heels. The look was casual yet slightly flirtatious.

"I look slutty," I said.

"No, you don't," Dana said, fixing my jacket collar, "you look younger and gorgeous. I'm wearing something similar." She wore tight black jeans, a sparkly top, a jean jacket, and low heels. "James even picked it out for me."

"Where is he?" I asked.

"He has a case," she shrugged. "Said he might join us later. At least then you'll finally meet him."

"When was the last time you were at a club?"

"Jeez, I can't remember. Maybe ten, fifteen years ago."

"The last time I went out, the kids hadn't been born yet." I laughed. It was absurd that I was going out.

"You aren't dead yet. We'll definitely see people our age; it won't just be people in their twenties. Now come or we're going to be late." Dana grabbed my hand.

"Maybe I shouldn't go," I said hesitantly, chewing on my thumbnail. "This feels wrong."

Dana slowly shook her head. "I've been telling you for a while that Ethan had interests elsewhere, but you didn't listen to me. You know there's something up with him. I mean, which male in his right mind doesn't want you every night?" she asked rhetorically. "Seriously though," she started. Her expression scared me. "I've seen this happen many times; men and women come to me with this gut feeling and it's always right. I'm telling you, Ethan has a girlfriend on the side."

"It's because I'm not the easiest person to live with."

"Don't make excuses for his behavior. Nobody is perfect. If it weren't difficult, it wouldn't be worth it. We all have to work on our relationships every single day. All of us. Nobody is exempt from putting in effort. You've confronted Ethan, and you tried, but he is the one who has made little effort. It's time for you to move forward and enjoy yourself; do something for you. Now that someone has an interest in you, go with the flow and see if you like it. If you still feel uncomfortable, then we come home. Okay?" Dana wrapped her arms around me for a comforting hug. "I wouldn't normally advocate for someone to cheat, but from what you've told me about Ethan and my experience. Just do it. If he is, why can't you."

"You're right," I said, nodding. "It just feels terrible. It's not like me. I already feel guilty when I've done nothing."

"I know," Dana said, kissing my cheek. "It shows what a good person you are and have a conscience."

I smiled, but it didn't reach my eyes. Dana was right, but I couldn't shake the uncomfortable feeling.

"Now let's get you to the party." She grinned.

"You're excited."

"I know; it's because it's a break in my routine. You forget I'm also a wife with a boring routine; I also need something exciting to happen once in a while." She winked. "And right now, I'm with my friend, and we're going to have a wonderful time dancing and drinking."

We went in Dana's car to a warehouse near Chicago's industrial area; I never knew this place existed until Tom had told me about it. The club had no name, was unsearchable, yet it was popular via word of mouth. Strobe lights filled the starless sky, reminding me of the Batman signal, calling everyone over. People gathered near a food truck, while others waited patiently in line to enter the venue.

Tom had texted me he'd wait for us by the entrance. Narrowing my eyes, I spotted a tall man with broad shoulders and neat hair. He was speaking to two women, who nodded and wrote something on their clipboards.

Dana was already out of the car and banging on my window. "You're supposed to get out," she smirked, opening my door. "We can't take the car in with us."

"Haha," I said, chuckling. "You're funny." I climbed out and closed the door while Dana pressed the button on her fob, her BMW beeped and locked.

She slipped her arm through mine, and we walked with purpose. The tall guy turned around as if sensing our approach and focused on me.

"I've had limited interactions with him," Dana whispered. "I hope his intentions are pure and genuine and he makes you happy."

I smiled at her. "I hope so too."

"You made it," Tom said, closing the distance quickly and reaching for my face, kissing my cheek chastely. "Hey, Dana."

"Hey, yourself stranger," she said. "Why didn't you tell me you had the hots for my friend?"

I glared at her.

Tom smiled, ignoring Dana's question. "Right through here," he said, reaching for my hand and leading the way.

"Oooh, I like it when we get special treatment," Dana

said by my ear so only I could hear her and slipped her smaller hand into mine.

The music boomed in my ears, the heat from the crowded room knocked my breath away, and all I wanted to do was cover my ears and sit outside.

"I've booked us a table," Tom yelled as he led us up a flight of stairs with a large VIP sign against the wall and the biggest bouncer I'd ever seen stood with arms the size of my waist. My jaw dropped slightly as we approached the mountain of a man.

Tom said something to the bouncer, who nodded, narrowing his eyes at Dana and then me, making me squirm. He had that fresh-out-of-the-marines vibe, and I wondered whether he killed people who got out of line in the club or just broke bones.

The bouncer nodded, allowing us entrance into the VIP section. Tom let go of my hand when we reached the reserved table and helped me sit, then he helped Dana.

"I'm just going to the bar," Tom yelled over the music and disappeared.

"Wow," Dana said, surveying with admiration. "He's really trying to impress you. Do you know how much it costs to book a table here?"

I shook my head. "No, how much?"

"Some of my clients have come here, and let's just say Tom must have something on the side when he's not a personal trainer, because it's at least a thousand and that's before the drinks," she said.

I didn't know how much personal trainers made but I agreed with Dana, Tom had to have a second job to afford coming here. The clientele all dressed and behaved like trust fund kids.

Tom arrived with an expensive bottle of champagne in

an ice bucket. Behind him, a waitress appeared and set glasses on the table and six shots filled with blue liquid.

"Do you always go all out when you bring ladies here?" I asked nervously when he sat beside me.

"Only you, Pam." Tom kissed my cheek. He was smooth, possibly too smooth, or he really liked me and was serious about us; it confused me. One moment I thought he was serious about me, but then he'd say something, and it sounded rehearsed, like he'd said the same thing to every woman he slept with. "Plus, I'm good friends with the owner." He winked. "I don't always ask for favors but tonight is different. I want to spoil you," he said, smiling.

It happened again; I wanted to melt into a puddle at his feet under his penetrating glare. This man was saying all the right words and doing everything perfectly. I felt safe beside him, wanted to hold his hand, wanted to kiss him, wanted to do anything he asked. The butterflies flapped their wings inside my stomach, and I couldn't stop grinning.

"Here." Tom handed me a shot and clinked his glass against mine, then Dana. When Dana clinked her glass against mine, she spilled half of it.

"Sorry," Dana said, licking her fingers. "Bottom's up!"

We downed our shots; at first the taste was bitter then sweet, but it burned all the way down my throat. I shuddered as goosebumps crawled across my skin.

"I haven't had shots since my twenties," I said and giggled. The blue alcohol went straight to my head; my face flushed.

Tom poured a glass of champagne each for us, followed by another round of clinking glasses without spilling. I savored the tiny bubbles of fresh champagne, smacking my lips together in satisfaction. The beat of the music vibrated under my feet and in time with my heart. My face was not as hot as I sipped the cool liquid.

A man came up behind Tom, tapping him on his shoulder. He set his glass down, stood, and hugged the man. Tom's back was facing me, so all I could see was the man's dark curly hair and black clothing. Turning towards Dana, whose eyes had widened, she mouthed the word *drugs* and shrugged.

"I don't know," I said, shaking my head. A nervousness settled in the pit of my stomach. Drugs. I hoped it wasn't recreational drugs. Dana was a P.I. and her husband was a detective. This was bad. This was very bad.

Tom sat down and rested his fist on my thigh. "Not sure if you've ever partied before?" He said *partied* in such a way that he might have meant something completely different from what I thought.

"What do you mean?" I asked, needing more information.

Tom opened his hand, palm up, with six purple tablets.

"I'd never tried anything like that before," I said, staring at his hand and then at Dana.

"I won't have," Dana said. "If you want to try it, then try." She jerked her chin toward the pills. "You have no responsibilities this weekend, but if you're uncomfortable, then don't do it. If you need me, I'm right here."

"Are you sure?" Tom asked Dana.

"Yeah," she said. "My detective husband will join us soon, and I don't want to put anyone in a position where they feel uncomfortable. This way, you two can enjoy yourselves, and I won't go through a divorce." She grinned. "Don't worry about me; it's her you need to focus your energy on," she winked and downed the rest of her champagne.

My stomach dropped to my toes thinking about taking recreational drugs. I never imagined doing anything like this ever, and here I was about to have with a man I liked.

"Start with one, and I'll do the same." Tom held out two tablets, pocketing the rest. "If you're having fun and want to try another, they're in my pocket."

"What will happen to me?" I asked, staring at the pills.

"My dealer only supplies the best. They've improved the recipe these days with hardly any side effects apart from dry mouth. All you must do is drink water throughout the evening. Once the effects start, it will give you a rush like you've never had before along with a surge in energy. You'll dance, laugh, and just have a good time," he said, swallowing his tablet and downing his champagne. "There's nothing you need to worry about."

It worried me. I didn't know how the drug would affect me or whether I'd make a fool of myself. I glanced at Dana, who smiled.

"Try it," Dana said. "If you need me, I'm right here." Her words comforted me.

Then I glanced at Tom, whose smile brightened his face and made me feel as if I were the only woman in the bubble he'd created for us. These feelings were dangerous because right now I wanted to make him happy, which meant I'd do anything for him. This was wrong, yet I wanted to do it. Again, I had conflicting thoughts and emotions.

My whole life I'd been a good girl. I always did what Ethan expected of me without question, putting my family first, and I tried to be a better person every single day. All I wanted was an evening where I could let loose and enjoy myself, and with no repercussions. I wanted to do something for me.

I exhaled a sharp breath and shrugged. Grabbing the

last pill, I placed it on my tongue and shuddered from the bitter taste, swallowing it with champagne. I gagged, choked on it but got it down, finishing my champagne.

"Let me know how it feels," Dana said. "Pass me the champagne."

Chapter Ten

PAM

I FELT the music in my veins. The beat travelled from my toes, up my legs and spine, into my shoulders, down my arms and out my fingers. My body moved without my needing to think as the music took control. I was there, dancing, yet floating. The lights were hypnotic, and the bodies dancing on the floor created a soft warmth one could almost touch. I wanted to reach out and cuddle in that warmth like it was a soft blanket.

Tom danced behind me, his large muscular hands caressed my hips as he pulled me closer into him while we danced. He pulled me even closer against him, feeling his honed body against my back. I leaned into him as we swayed to the beat. His lips hovered near my neck, his breath hot against my skin, sending waves of sensations down my spine as all the hair on my body stood on end. I shivered in pleasurable anticipation.

Tom moved his hand from the curve of my waist to the front and below my belly button. His fingers spread wide and edged closer to my pelvic area as he pulled me into him.

I raised my arms above my head and combed my fingers through his short hair. The pulsating music made us move as one. His body was hot against mine. The rhythm of the music beat against us as we gave in to the universe.

I opened my eyes; the VIP area blurred around the edges. Tiny spiraling ribbons fell to the floor, dangling from the ceiling. A star appeared behind the bar, contracting with the beat of the music. The barman danced on the counter, his arms and legs held by strings as the puppet master high above made him move. The walls breathed like lungs, and the patterns slithered up and down like snakes. The large portraits on the walls changed color as the paint melted off the canvas, dripping to the floor. Paint splashed against people dancing nearby, absorbing them, and taking them into the portraits on the walls. Confused about what was real and what wasn't, I thought it best not to think at all and to let go, to enjoy the feel of the music, the drug coursing through my veins, and the man behind me.

Dana waved, her hand visible in the sea of moving bodies. A tall man with chestnut-colored hair held her possessively. He smiled in greeting. Then they laughed and kissed and shared a drink. He had to be… I bit my lower lip trying to remember her husband's name, but it floated out of my head.

I blinked, and Julia's face materialized out of the crowd. Her blonde hair beautifully styled, like she'd just stepped out of a salon. Someone as beautiful as her should be on the cover of a fashion magazine. She stared at me and her beauty faded, leaving behind an older version filled with wrinkles, discoloration, and dark, sunken rings under her eyes. Julia smiled and waved, then turned towards the dark-haired man beside her, and wrapped her arms around his neck. I did a slow blink, and she became a faceless body on the dance floor. Another blink and they disappeared.

I blinked again, glancing at everyone around me as their heads popped and became faceless bodies. Nausea bubbled to the surface, and I needed to burp or something but was too afraid I'd throw up. I turned around in Tom's embrace and glanced up at his smiling dark eyes that were burning a hole in my face. His lips parted as he neared, brushing his lips against mine.

Fireworks exploded inside my body, hot, warm, happy, feel-good emotions crashed through me one after the other as I melded into Tom. Our hands roamed over each other's clothing and then underneath as I couldn't get enough of his silky skin beneath my fingers. I wanted more of Tom, more than I'd ever wanted anyone in my life. Tom's hand cupped my breast while the other darted inside my jeans and cupped my ass cheek, squeezing. My core clenched at the stimulation, and I needed more.

We danced, kissed, touched and laughed. I couldn't remember having had this much fun before. Soon after school, I'd started working and never had the chance to embrace my wild side. Afraid of making a mistake, I never took a chance on anything and did nothing risky; nothing like this. And I was happy. I hadn't been this happy in a long time and relished in that fact. I also decided that from tonight, I'd do more for myself; whatever that meant.

The rest of the evening flew by with a mixture of sensual touching, bright lights, hips moving, skin crawling, faces changing, lips tasting, eyes flirting, colors dripping, and lots of alcohol and water.

Sometime during the night, I didn't know when since I

hadn't looked at my phone, Tom gave me the other two pills. He placed the purple pills on my tongue, held a glass to my mouth to drink, and then everything went black.

———

THE DARKNESS FADED, and I found myself straddling Tom's waist fully clothed, rocking into him while he had his hands around my neck, stopping the air from flowing into my lungs. I ground into him, feeling his hardness pressed against me. No air. Then, his mouth covered my breast, and he bit down hard, tearing pleasurable moans from my mouth. Pure ecstasy flooded my system, and blackness swallowed me whole.

I blinked, and we were kissing. His lips were soft against mine, his tongue playing with mine. His hands burned my skin where he touched. I ached for him to be inside me and moaned during our kiss. I blinked as the ecstasy coursed through my veins and the darkness neared.

The next moment I was standing naked against the wall, and Tom's fingers were pumping inside me. The orgasm was about to tear through me, forcing me to hold on to him. Another slow blink, and then the blackness enveloped us.

Tom was naked and above me; his face peppered with sweat. He thrusted hard, like he was about to push through me. The sensations rocking into me were building, and I was about to scream my release. Tom's continuous movement was like nothing I'd ever felt before, and I didn't want him to stop.

I smiled as I watched Tom pump into me, and it was as if it was the first time for me. He was so different from Ethan.

Tom grunted, pulling my attention towards him as his

eyes rolled into the back of his head. My vision tunneled. The darkness surrounded us.

Then nothing.

Chapter Eleven

PAM

MY HEAD THROBBED, and the pounding intensified as I stretched my limbs. I wiggled my fingers and, instead of feeling the bedsheet, a silky substance dripped between my fingers. I brought my hand to my face and opened my eyes. In front of me were my blurry red fingers. The more I blinked, the more I saw. It was my hand in front of my face, my fingers, but the red substance was foreign. Glancing at the ceiling, I couldn't understand whose dark ceiling this was because my house had white ceilings.

I tried to remember last night and what I'd been doing. I was dancing and drinking and having fun, but then... darkness.

Why were these ceilings dark?

Where was I?

Why was there red liquid on my hand?

I bolted upright to view my surroundings, the red liquid dripping down my back and bum, but I couldn't think of that now as I glanced around. At the foot of the bed sat a brown leather couch facing a flat-screen TV on the face brick wall that didn't reach the ceiling. To my left were large windows with streams of sunlight coming inside, warming my naked skin. To my right was a door to the bathroom, and instead of a door to the bedroom was an opening revealing the open planned living space. It was a studio apartment. I was inside someone's apartment. In someone's bed. And I was naked. I shivered again as the red silk sheets slipped off my breasts but didn't bother covering up. There were more important things to do than to be embarrassed by my nakedness.

A numbness crept over my body as my mind tried to piece together what had happened last night; my clean finger touched my lips instinctively. There was touching, and lots of kissing. Drugs, there were drugs, and lots of alcohol. And sex, I'd been with someone other than my husband.

Oh, my gods. I had sex with someone else as bits and pieces of the visions of what we did floated into my mind. *But who?*

A cool wind caressed my skin, and I shuddered as I thought about the implications of my actions. I scrunched the sheets in my hands, and the squishy liquid oozed between my fingers. I glanced down and stared at the red substance. My mind couldn't process what I was looking at; red juice in bed, red silk sheets, wetness on my fingers, and more of the wetness all over the sheets. I swallowed the lump in my throat as I lifted the sheet, the red, thick liquid dripping onto my legs. Bringing my hand near my face to smell it and I coughed, sucking in more of the coppery odor, and I gagged. Whatever I drank last night threatened to repeat itself, and I swallowed hard.

I turned to the naked person beside me and gently

pushed my dry index finger against his shoulder blade, but he didn't stir.

He's naked. He's naked. He's naked. I thought to myself as I covered him with the sheet again, but I needed him to wake up. He had to give me answers. I needed him to tell me we were okay, that neither of us were hurt.

"Hello. Tom?" I said, but all I heard was the whir of the air conditioner. I gently pushed against his shoulder blade with the palm of my hand, leaving my bloody handprint on his back. "Shit, sorry. Wake up?" I whispered, my tone bordering on panic. "You need to wake up, Tom. Please, please, please, wake up."

He didn't respond.

"No, no, no." The walls closed in on me. My flesh heated as ice moved through my veins. I threw the silk sheets completely off my body to cool my naked flesh.

"Shit," I cried. "Tom?" He didn't move. I was married, and the person beside me was not my husband, and he wasn't moving.

Another cold sensation washed over me, bringing me out of my drug and alcohol -induced hangover and into reality. When I threw off the silk sheets, I had uncovered the man beside me. His naked ass perfect, the only flaw was he didn't move.

"Please wake up," I whimpered. The reality of my situation sinking in.

If this red liquid was his blood, where was he bleeding from?

I tried to think about what had happened the previous night, bit my nail and tasted the copper liquid instead. Bile rose in my throat as last night's shots threatened to come back up.

Naked, confused, and unsure, I surveyed the room again.

The studio apartment was neat and tidy, with dark colors and leather. No woman had ever lived here. There were no flowers, no colors and no photos. I glanced at the person in bed, at his brown hair and profile. Leaning over his unmoving body, I tried moving him, but he was too heavy.

"Tom? Get up!"

I climbed out of bed and walked around to the other side to see if Tom was okay. I knew he wasn't, but I still had to check. The silk sheets had bunched under his chest, and I carefully tugged him free of them. Blood splashed onto his chest and pooled beneath him. He didn't stir. I couldn't tell where his blood began, and the red bedsheets ended. Everything was red.

"Tom?" I cried, falling to my knees. My naked body pressed against the side of the bed as I reached for his lifeless face, his beautiful face. Tom was one of those heavenly creatures who were perfect both inside and out. He had spoken to me about how he had transformed his life, and how he wanted to make amends. He wanted to be a better person. That's what I wanted too, transformation. And that's what I went after, but I didn't want this. I wanted nothing bad to happen to Tom.

I stared at Tom's body and squinted. There was only one cut on his body; his neck. I couldn't believe so much blood came out of him from such a minor cut; it must've hit a large artery and done with a knife I couldn't see. I spun around, searching for it on the bedside tables and floor. Something glinted on my side of the bed. The early morning sun highlighted the silver glow. The knife was under my pillow. I wanted to reach for it but knew better.

Shivering in the cool air, I knew the best thing was to call the police. *But.* It looked bad. I was married and, in someone else's bed, and that someone else was dead. I was the only person here; the police wouldn't bother looking at anyone else.

I already looked guilty.

The police would draw my blood, have it tested and would know I took illegal recreational drugs. Ethan would find out about everything. I'd go to jail and lose Ethan. I'd lose my kids. Nobody would believe me that someone else had done this. There was no way I would hurt someone I was falling in love with. There was no way I could've done this.

All I wanted was a good time out, but... then... I tried to think... I couldn't recall what had happened after Tom gave me those two pills.

Everything was blank.

Maybe I killed him. I thought, remembering reading an article where some pharmaceuticals could alter someone's brain so much that they'd do something they wouldn't have done sober. No, I didn't want to believe it. There's no way I would hurt someone like this. I stared down at Tom's bloody body. *It wasn't me.*

I walked through the apartment searching for my handbag, finding it with my clothing on the kitchen counter where broken glass and a broken bottle of champagne lay on the tiled floor. I tiptoed over the glass and spilled champagne, reaching over the counter to retrieve my bag. My heart almost sank to my toes when I couldn't find my cellphone when I noticed it had fallen on the floor and surrounded by glass. There was only one person I could reach out to for help.

Chapter Twelve

PAM

I DIDN'T KNOW where I was, and I desperately needed help. I first searched for a broom, which I found in a closet where Tom kept his cleaning materials, and with the handle pushed the cellphone out of the glass. Crouching to pick it up, I flinched when something burned. With my phone in my hand, I hopped backwards and lifted my foot to pull the piece of glass sticking out. Blood sprayed everywhere, and I groaned; another mess I needed to clean up, but I'd worry about that later.

I opened the map app on my phone so that I could send a pin location to Dana. I stared at the map, noting we were only a few blocks away from the health club. A lump formed at the back of my throat; I was near home. A home that was empty; neither my husband nor children would be there, and none had left me messages. At least I didn't have to lie to them about where I was or what I was doing.

I exhaled a shaky breath; nobody was looking for me. As much as it relieved me, it also saddened me. I was all alone.

Glancing down at my blood-soaked skin, I wanted to get

clean. Seeing myself in the mirror covered in Tom's blood would haunt me for the rest of my life. His blood caked my right-hand side, and it stuck to my hair.

I turned on the shower taps, allowing the hot water to wash away my sins. Using Tom's soap, I scrubbed my body clean and his shampoo for my hair. Tears streamed down my face while doing so, because all I smelled was him all over me. When I used his towel, I smelled him there too.

Wearing last night's clothing was not an option, so I opened Tom's closet, reaching for a t-shirt and pants small enough that fit me. While getting dressed, I kept glancing at Tom, hoping he'd wake up, but he didn't. He just lay there with his eyes open, staring at the floor; it was unnerving.

Quickly, I pulled on Tom's clothing, and started cleaning the kitchen. I picked up the larger glass pieces, cut myself on one of them and cursed. Holding my finger under the cold water tap until the blood stopped flowing. I pulled a few tissues out of the box and wrapped my finger.

I flinched when the doorbell chimed. Peering through the peephole, I saw Dana and opened the door.

"Babe!" Dana said, hugging me. The moment Dana pulled me into a comforting embrace, I broke down into a sob. "No, don't cry. Now tell me what happened and why I'm here? Your message was cryptic."

"I don't know," I cried. "I don't remember what happened after I took those two pills." Letting go of Dana, I grabbed more tissues to dry my face.

"Oh no," Dana shrieked when she saw the kitchen floor. Her eyes darted from the broken glasses to the blood on the floor to me. "Did he do this to you?" She reached for my bloodied hand. "Did he hurt you?"

"No, I just cut myself trying to clean up, and I cut my foot when I reached for my phone. But…," I sobbed, breaking down again. "I think I've done something bad, Dana. Very, very bad," I mumbled, pointing towards the bedroom. "It wasn't me."

"What's wrong?" Dana said, traversing further inside the apartment.

"Come," I said, closing the front door.

Dana stopped in the doorway and stared. She said nothing, didn't move, just stared. She slowly turned to face me. "What happened, Pam?" she asked, arching both eyebrows. Dread filled her tone. "Did you shower?" Her eyes widened when she saw my wet hair, and the baggy clothing. "Are you wearing his clothes, and then you started cleaning?"

I covered my mouth with my hands. "I know this looks bad, but I woke up covered in his blood, and I freaked out." Pushing past her, I entered the room and pointed at the pillow I slept on. "I didn't kill him, Dana. You must believe me. The knife is here. Why would I stab him and place the knife under my head? Why would I kill him and then continue sleeping beside him? None of this makes sense, Dana. Please help me," I said, my voice raised. "I didn't do this."

"I need to phone Donnie and James—"

"No!" I yelled. "Please, you can't."

She lowered her hand holding her cellphone. "Pam, this is a crime scene, and you're making me an accomplice."

Swallowing my cry, I stepped closer to her. "I'm sorry. I don't know what I'm doing. All I know is I'm scared. I didn't do this. I couldn't hurt anyone like this. You must believe me."

"That's why you must leave the evidence alone and let the police handle it. Let them get the biological and trace evidence and test it. If they do their job, and you're innocent, you have nothing to worry about."

"But who would do such a thing and then…" I glanced at Tom. "…frame me." My voice sounded strained and hollow; I didn't recognize myself. I wiped tears off my face. "Why me?"

"I don't know, but you should've called the police the moment you woke up." Dana paced, squeezing the phone in her hand. "Wipe nothing just grab your stuff and let's go. The sooner we're out of this mess, the better. The cops need to handle this." She rubbed her temples. "I need to phone James and tell him—"

"No, don't!" I yelled, reaching for her.

"Back away," Dana said, raising her hand. "We might be friends, but this is a crime scene, and right now I don't know what to believe; stay there and don't touch me."

"I'm sorry," I said, averting my eyes, blinking back tears. My chin trembled.

"It's okay," she continued. "James saw you with Tom last night. We all know you were together. You are the prime suspect, anyway. The sooner we get them down here, the sooner they can clear you, the better for you."

My world came crashing down in that moment. Everything I lived for destroyed. I panicked, because that's what innocent *and* guilty people did. We panicked, and we ran. I needed to get away. I needed to solve this because once they arrested me, nobody would help me. Nobody would care that I was innocent, and they wouldn't be looking for the true killer. Based on Ethan's behavior of late, he would leave me in jail. But what I did in bringing Dana into this was wrong; I shouldn't have called her.

"I'm sorry for putting you in this situation. I didn't mean to," I said, glancing around the room. I snapped pictures of every part of the room. Then I moved towards the kitchen and collected my handbag. I grabbed a bag and stuffed my dress and shoes inside, along with anything else that belonged to me.

"No, wait, what are you doing? That's evidence," Dana said, grabbing my wrist. "Leave it; it needs to be processed."

I threw the dress and shoes on the floor. "We must get out of here," I said, glancing nervously at her. "Please know that I didn't do this. I hope you're in my corner, but I'd understand if you weren't. Let me leave so that I can figure out who's doing this to me. I need to find out why." I squeezed my eyes tight. "Going to jail isn't an option for me, Dana. I'll die in there."

She let go of my wrist. "I don't think you did this," she said gently, glancing around. "Okay, this is what you must do." Her tone was serious. "Get as much cash as you can. Don't go home. You need to vanish for a few days. Let everyone think you're dead, too. Send your pictures to the cloud. Memorize my number, buy a burner phone, and throw your old phone away. Never tell me or anyone where you are. I'll help you figure this out."

A knot formed in my throat, and I couldn't swallow or blink. "Thank you." I smiled, and the tears fell, wiping them away with the back of my hand. "I love my kids, and I'm afraid if I get sent away, I'll never see them again. Ethan will take them away. They may never know what really happened; I need to make sure the truth comes out."

"I know," she whispered. "If I woke up in something like this, I'd panic too. I don't think you're capable of something like this. Now go," she said, glancing around. She pulled her sleeve over her hand and wiped the areas she touched. "I was never here." She headed for the door. "Do you know whether there are cameras in his apartment or around the building?"

I shrugged. "I don't remember anything, Dana. One

would think having mind-blowing sex with someone you'd remember, but I don't. I remember nothing."

"Okay," she grabbed my elbow. "Do you have everything that was in your handbag?"

I nodded, looking at the contents. "I think so."

"Let's get out of here."

Chapter Thirteen

DANA

THE DARK LIQUID swirled in my mug, the aroma pleasant, yet I'd lost my desire to drink it. It was times like these when I missed my old partner, Marc, but those days were long gone along with the man who almost killed me. Marc had retired and was living his best life. While I had my private investigating service in Chicago.

I didn't want to risk writing my thoughts down in case James found my notebook, even though I always kept it at the office. But I needed the timeline of the events last night. I needed to figure out what had happened to Tom and who was trying to frame Pam.

I needed to tell James what had happened but couldn't risk it yet. I hated that I had to keep this from him. Sighing, I sat upright.

My client stepped out of the bathroom, wiping smudged makeup off her face. "Thank you, Dana," Tilly said, sitting across from me once more. "You've saved me from making one of the biggest mistakes of my life." She retrieved her cellphone and opened her banking app. "There," she said happily, "paid."

My cellphone chimed, letting me know the money was in my account. "Only a pleasure. I'm thrilled you know about this before marrying him."

"Totally." She leaned against the chair back and sighed. Tilly was engaged to a love-bombing jerk who manipulated her and made her think she was crazy. He also wanted to marry her without a prenup, which her father said no to for obvious reasons.

"I can't believe I almost married a monster. I mean, he changed his personality to hook me, to get me attached to him," she shook her head. "Then he did the whole hot and cold thing, making me feel unworthy, only for him to swoop in and give me short-lived affection. I feel so stupid."

"Don't," I said. "He knew what he was doing, and he did it on purpose to get you and then your money."

"I feel sorry for the women before and after me, if only there's a registry women could update and search before dating a guy. Imagine. Then we can see if his name is on it before agreeing to a date. You might lose business though." She laughed.

"Unfortunately, something like that isn't legal, and the men could sue for a variety of reasons. But I understand the appeal. It would be useful."

"Let me go," Tilly said, standing. "I have lunch with my dad."

I stood and opened the door for her. "Enjoy the rest of your Saturday." I closed the door behind her, locking it. I had no other clients today and would use the time to figure out what happened last night.

I glanced at the clock on the wall. It was almost noon;

James and Donnie should be at the crime scene already. While they were there, I'd go to the warehouse.

Chapter Fourteen

DANA

TODAY THE WAREHOUSE looked like every other deserted building in the industrial area. The only sign something might have happened last night was the litter on the ground, the cigarette butts, and the empty alcohol bottles lining the face brick wall.

I parked in front near the entrance and locked my car. The large wooden doors were unlocked when I tried the handle. "Hello?" I called as I entered. "Anyone here?"

"We're closed," a man yelled back. "Get out before I call the cops." I saw his bald head first as he stomped around the corner. He stopped dead when he saw me, the lines between his eyes deepening. "I recognize you." He pointed a thick finger at me.

"I was here last night with friends," I said. "We need your help. Do you recognize him?" I raised my cellphone and showed him a picture I had taken of Pamela and Tom. "Do you remember seeing them last night?"

Recognition flickered in the man's eyes, and he nodded. "I know Tom very well. Not so much his lady friend though.

But I saw them dancing last night." The smile on his face widened. "What did Tom do this time that you're looking for him?"

His comment surprised me. "Why would you say that? What has Tom done before?"

He sighed. "Who are you and why are you asking about Tom?" His tone changed from friendly to suspicious.

"I'm a private investigator and something has happened. I'd like to get a better understanding of who Tom is." I thought it best not to share any information about his death, leaving that for James and Donnie to handle. Tom was a personal trainer at the gym, yet last night he showed a different side of himself; a drug user, possibly friends with the wrong crowd, and had an enemy who wanted him dead.

The man stared at me as if he knew something but wasn't sure about sharing it.

"Please," I pleaded, "if you know anything about Tom that could help me solve this, I'd appreciate it if you could share that with me."

"Listen, I need to do some admin. Follow me to the office, and I'll tell you what I know about the guy." He spun on his heel and headed inside. "Name is Ben," he said, disappearing into the dark cavernous room.

I followed Ben, keeping my hand on my gun, which I kept under my jacket in its shoulder holster. I didn't know this man, and I was following him inside an empty building by myself. Although I vaguely remembered seeing him last night, but I couldn't be certain. There were so many people I could've mistaken him for someone else. We passed the female bathroom and ascended a flight of stairs hidden behind black curtains. There was only one room up here that overlooked the dance floor and bar area.

I entered the office behind Ben, taken aback by the stench of alcohol, sweat, and old smoke. The black floor was sticky beneath my feet, but what caught my attention was the dusty plastic plant in the corner near the door. The room could use a real plant to help clean the air.

"Okay," Ben said, sitting in a chair held together with duct tape and behind an old wooden desk. He motioned for me to sit in the white plastic chair opposite him. I didn't really want to sit so close to him, but I wanted information on Tom, and sat down. The chair was uncomfortable and creaked beneath my weight. I hoped it wouldn't break if I shifted.

Ben scratched his bald head, sighed, leaned back in his chair, and rested his hands on his stomach. "Tom used to sell drugs in my club, and sometimes he'd pick up women and take them home with him. Sometimes the women would complain because they couldn't remember what had happened to them. Now," he raised both hands in mock surrender, "I'm not saying Tom did anything wrong. All I'm saying is he has a reputation for doing something the women didn't like. According to him, all the women gave him consent. He has pictures of them sitting happily with him, sometimes clothed, sometimes not, and all of them gave him consent."

My stomach tightened into knots. I didn't expect to hear this about Tom, which made me wonder if he did something to Pam that she didn't want to do, and she unknowingly reacted negatively to the drugs and killed him in self-defense.

I was relieved I took nothing from Tom last night, or I might have been in bed beside James not knowing what I was doing. Or worse, I could've been between Tom and Pamela with a knife in my hand. The possibilities for destruction were endless, especially not knowing what was in that drug.

"And his business partner would sometimes go after the same women and do the same thing."

"Who is his business partner?" I vaguely remembered the man wearing black Tom had hugged before showing us the drugs.

"His name is Lucky. Dodgy fucker if you ask me. He isn't welcome inside my club, but somehow, he gets inside. When I find out who is letting him in, he's out on the street too. That boy brings dangerous drugs here. The last thing I need is a reputation for having drugs floating here that's causing harm to my patrons." He shook his head. "I don't need that kind of heat."

"Has anyone reacted badly to the drug?"

"Not in my club, but I've heard from these women that they didn't feel well afterwards."

The knot in my stomach grew larger, making me nauseous. The more I learned about Tom, the more I wished Pamela didn't know him at all, but I needed to dig and find out what happened to clear her name.

"Do you know where I can find Lucky?"

"He has an apartment a few blocks away. Can't remember the name of the place, but it has a large squirrel spray-painted on the side of the building. You can't miss it."

"Thanks," I said, making a note. "When did Tom stop dealing drugs?"

"Probably a year or two ago. He finished his studies and started working at the gym as a personal trainer. He tried not doing the drugs he sold, but I know he fell off the wagon every now and then, especially when he was around Lucky. That boy is bad news. The two of them together is worse. I was happy when Tom got out and cleaned up, but

Lucky," he shook his head, "Lucky can't seem to get his act together."

"Do you have any contact details of the women Tom or Lucky may have hurt?" If I could get testimony from someone other than Pam, it could help her case.

"Nah, man, nothing." Ben thought for a moment, then opened a drawer. "I had a waitress who worked for me in the VIP section. One day Elizabeth was chirpy, and everything was going well; the next she was gone. She didn't say goodbye or collect her check. My bartender said Tom had gotten to her, then I knew I'd never hear from her again. I did reach out to her, but she didn't reply."

"Can I have her number?"

"Hmm, it must be here," he rummaged through the same drawer and pulled out an employee card. I copied her details.

My mouth twisted in disgust. "How many women do you think Tom has done this to?"

"Not sure, but I remember them talking about the things he got up to inside the club. It makes me sick to think about it."

"How many?" I pushed.

"He'd have sex with three women a night here at the club and still take one home. It's the one he took home you should really be concerned about though."

Nausea bubbled at the thought of what his body count was. Poor Pam, she was just another notch on his belt; a conquest, nothing but an easy lay.

"If I had to guess, it could be hundreds," Ben added. "Sometimes these boys just don't give a shit about anyone but themselves. It's like they need to fuck their problems away, yet all they're doing is causing harm. I'd find so many used condoms in bathroom stalls or in dark corners on

Saturday morning. At least Tom was responsible not to spread diseases or impregnate any of them. The last thing he needs is a smaller version of himself running around."

I made a mental note to tell Pam to get tested; *just in case.*

"Do you think Tom has an addictive personality?"

"Oh yeah, for sure. Alcohol, sex, drugs, and even exercise; he has emotions he needs to numb and block out. I wanted to feel sorry for the guy, but not after hearing about all the shit he got up to. He deserves what's coming to him."

I must've spaced out for a moment because Ben cleared his throat and grabbed a stack of papers from a tray.

"Thanks for answering my questions," I said, standing. "I'll see myself out."

"When you see Tom, tell him he's no longer welcome. If he comes here, I'll have him arrested."

I didn't bother answering Ben and exited his office, descending the stairs slowly as I glanced around, but instead of leaving I walked along the black curtain that hid the stairs and office. There were a couple of emergency exits that were locked from the inside, and an unlocked door that led to the fire escape outside.

I parted the black curtain to see where I was, noting that the VIP section was a few steps away. This was how Lucky had gained entrance last night when he dropped off the drugs for Tom.

I circled back the way I came, checked the bar area and then headed for the exit. As I approached the door, a man entered. "Hey, what are you doing here?" he asked, stopping in the doorway, blocking me from leaving.

"Had a meeting with Ben quickly." I thumbed over my shoulder.

"Oh, okay," he said, stepping to one side, holding the

door open for me. He watched me leave. His eyes were so brown they seemed black, his brown beard neatly combed and oiled, and his brown hair tied in a man bun. He wore a red and black flannel shirt, looking every bit like an axe-wielding woodcutter who belonged in the forest.

I climbed into my car and glanced back at the warehouse, and the *Woodcutter* continued watching me. I waved because that's all I could think of to do in the moment. Turning the ignition, my car roared to life, and I slowly merged with traffic.

It was lunchtime, and I'd eaten little all day, but after the conversation with Ben I'd lost my appetite. We didn't know Tom at all based on what I'd heard now. Even though Tom came across as a nice person, he was far from it. He drugged and sexually assaulted women, used drugs and sex as a weapon, and preyed upon the vulnerable. I didn't want to tell Pam any of this, but I had to.

I didn't know how I could find more of his victims without raising the alarm with Donnie and James. For now, the only person was the ex-employee, and I'd like to get a sense of what he did to her before I did anything else.

Chapter Fifteen

DANA

IT TOOK me fifteen minutes to find the squirrel painted on the side of the apartment building. There was no name listed anywhere, nor was there a visible street name. The streets had litter everywhere, and across the road, the homeless had erected tents. I hardly ever visited this side of Chicago because of how things had changed, and violent crime was on the rise.

I entered the building, glancing up the stairwell, wondering how I'd find Lucky when something caught my eye. The postboxes stood opposite the nonworking elevator, and I smiled when I saw Lucky's name on the number six postbox.

Relieved I didn't have to go up too many flights of stairs, I ran up the two flights, finding number six on the far side of the corridor. I knocked twice.

"Who is it?"

"My name is Dana. Ben told me where I could find you."

"Shit," he mumbled, and a glass crashed to the floor,

shattering. "I'll be there now." After five minutes of his cleaning up the broken glass, he opened the door. "Yeah? Why are you looking for me?" Lucky asked, standing in colorful shorts and a tight white vest. He scratched at his bushy red beard and narrowed his small eyes at me; I couldn't tell what color they were. He wore flip-flops, and his left big toe had blood on it.

"I'm a private investigator and would like to speak with you about Tom."

"Yeah? Why? What's that cunt gone and done now?" Lucky left the door open and entered the kitchen on the right to throw the broken glass away. "Come inside, just excuse the place. I wasn't exactly expecting company."

"No problem," I said, entering and closing the door behind me.

Lucky's apartment was messy and dirty. The cushions on the couch looked like he'd stabbed them, with their stuffing coming out, and there were empty beer bottles on the coffee table. The tiled floor desperately needed a mopping, and his kitchen was an explosion of grime and dirty dishes. I shuddered at the thought of cooking in there.

I waited for Lucky to settle down before asking him questions.

"So, what do you want to know about that dickhead?" he asked again, heading towards the couch.

"How long have you known Tom?"

Lucky sat on the two-seater. I pushed empty wrappers off the sofa and sat across from him.

"Let me see," he said, pondering. "Tom and I went to school together. He started…" he said, leaving his sentence hanging, glancing nervously at me.

"I know about the drugs," I said, encouraging him to continue.

"...dealing before me. It first started with weed, you know. It's the gateway drug to everything else. Then he started dealing in cocaine, and I joined him. With the money we made, we'd spend some of it on the same drugs we were selling. I got hooked on cocaine. Tom said his head was too strong to be addicted to anything, but he became addicted too; he even tried heroin. Now that stuff is bad." He shuddered. "I guess we've been at it ever since, or rather, I've continued. He stopped about a year or two ago, but he still dabbles now and then."

"And the women he uses?" I didn't think it was necessary to explain myself. Lucky was smart enough to know where I was going.

"Has one bitch finally come forward with proof?" He didn't look amused. "It was bound to bite Tom in the ass. The guy drugs them, fucks them, and leaves them feeling unsure about their reality. Dick moves, man."

"Why did he do it though? He isn't ugly, and I'm sure he can get any girl he wants without drugging them."

"See, that's just the thing about Tom. He has a cute boy next door look with his short hair, blue eyes, and naughty smile. The chicks loved his *innocent* look until he got his hooks in them. He can get any girl he desires, but I think somewhere down the line he got messed up badly. Took too many drugs, too much cocaine, too much heroin. Who the fuck knows? He also has big-dick energy, if you know what I mean. Maybe his ego got to him. Maybe one girl rejected him, and then he took revenge on all the rest." He shrugged. "Who knows, man? He's fucked in his head. He's even got a Body Count book; takes pictures of the women and writes about it like a fucking diary."

I couldn't believe what I was hearing, but at the same

time I could. Tom was a nasty piece of work packaged deceptively beautiful.

"Do you know where it is?" I needed to get my hands on that book.

"In his apartment somewhere." He fell silent for a moment. "Bookshelf. Maybe a secret compartment, but it's definitely there. I've seen him take it from there when he needed to brag; feed his ego."

I couldn't remember seeing a bookshelf in his apartment, but I had to get in there somehow and get that book. It might have information in there I could use to help Pam and find more victims.

"Did you hurt the women the same way? Do you have your own Body Count book?" I asked, remembering what Ben had told me about Lucky.

"Hell no, man," he said defensively, "and forget what that asshole Ben told you; he's a dick for even suggesting it. Now he's a dodgy fucker. And I never went after Tom's scraps. The women found *me* and asked for *my* help. I swear. I didn't touch them. They knew I was good friends with Tom, and when he ignored their calls and messages, they came to me. When he eventually saw them, he left them feeling like they were going crazy. I helped them fill in the gaps so that they could move on. Told them where to go for therapy, and to stay away from Tom. I then told Tom to stop, but the guy just couldn't; he was addicted to the rush of getting away with it. Addicted to the chase. The guy was addicted to everything."

"But he raped them?"

"It's a fine line. They *consented* to being with him; they just don't remember. He filmed this consent as proof and would deny ever drugging them. He'd say it was their guilty conscience for having sex with him, and they couldn't hold him accountable after the fact."

I shook my head in disgust. I couldn't believe what I was hearing; it was disgusting how he got their consent. It was a scary gray line he crossed. He was a predator of the worst kind.

"Do you have any of the girls' numbers so that I can speak with them?"

"Only a few." Lucky stood and fetched his cellphone. "Here," he said, showing me a list of five names and numbers. I wrote them down in my notebook. "Not sure if their numbers still work but you can try. It's been years. I wouldn't blame them if they changed it; it might be the only way they can get over what Tom did."

"Thanks," I said. "Anything else you can tell me about Tom?"

"He tried to get his life in order when he stopped the drugs and dealing. Went legit, you know. Became a personal trainer and all that. He wanted to sort his shit out. I knew he liked the one woman he was training. Can't remember her name, but he was with her last night at the warehouse. He kept going on and on about how he wants to change for her, and I sincerely hope he does. He needs a good woman in his life; I just hope she never finds out about his shady past or that Body Count book, because that can end in disaster." Lucky narrowed his eyes at me, then shook his head.

"Do you think he changed?"

He nodded. "It's been two years since he stopped fucking all the women and drugging them. I don't think he wanted to go back to his old ways. One evening he stopped by, and he was crying; he knew what he did was wrong. That he was fucked up. For the first time in his life, he felt guilt; he knew he wasn't a nice person. Sometimes he would love-bomb the women, fuck 'em, breadcrumb them, and then avoid them. Told me he had so much on his mind that the only thing that helped was fucking the women so hard he wanted to break them, tear them in two, make them scream in pain. He wanted to push his cock straight through them. He's fucked in the head; but I think it was just the drugs messing him up, you know. Sometimes drugs can alter a person's brain; their personality. Hell, I'm fucked up." He chuckled, but it sounded hollow, sad.

I didn't know what to say after hearing that. I'd never heard of someone wanting to fuck another person so hard before. It made me wonder what else went through Tom's mind.

"Thank you for sharing so much with me, Lucky," I said, wanting to leave; I'd heard enough for now. "I really appreciate your candor."

"I have my cross to bear," he said sadly, staring at the joint in his hands, "and I have a lot to atone for what I've done in my life. If I can help you and maybe some of the other women," he glanced up at me, "then that's what I'll do. You name it."

"And you still deal?" I stood and headed for the door.

He nodded, standing with me. His blue/green eyes glistened in the light. He hadn't brushed his short curly black hair in days. I didn't want to get too close to him but suspected he needed a shower.

"I tried getting a normal job in the kitchen cleaning dishes, but I have a record and well," he shrugged, "nobody wanted to hire me. So yeah, I'll do this until the day I die. Nothing else I can do. But I will say I only supply the cleanest and finest. No more of that other shit that hurts people. I swear."

"Here's my card if you think of something else about Tom."

"Why are you asking about him?" he asked, glancing at my card before placing it on the kitchen counter.

"Let's just say something happened to him, and I'm trying to piece things together."

"Did one bitch gut him?"

The look I gave him said it all.

"It was only a matter of time." He opened his front door. "If there's one person who I think might actually hurt Tom, is Elizabeth Marconi. They used to work together. She almost died and vowed to get back at him."

Chapter Sixteen

DANA

ELIZABETH MARCONI WAS a twenty-nine-year-old woman working at a coffee shop. She had short black/blue hair, the whitest eyebrows I'd ever seen, with the prettiest blue eyes. Although she had a nose and lip ring, it didn't detract from her strange natural beauty. Elizabeth was shorter than I and very skinny. I wanted to buy her a meal.

"Just give me five minutes," she said, making a latte for a customer.

"I'll be over there," I said, pointing at a table in the back. The coffee here was great. I sipped my cappuccino and watched the customers come in, buy their coffee and leave again while waiting for her.

After ten minutes, she finally approached. "Why do you want to speak with me?" she asked, sitting across from me. She leaned her elbows on the table; her collarbone stuck out, cheeks were gaunt, eyes sunken, and her fingers long and bony. Her youthful face had hard lines I could only attribute to terrible experiences.

"I want to ask you about Tom—"

"Fuck," she said, shaking her head and slowly getting up.

"Please," I said, grabbing her thin arm. "Tell me what he did to you."

"I can't," she said, yanking her arm free. "If I ever see that guy again, I'll kill him. I swear. I hate that guy. He's a narcissistic psycho who preys on women. He thinks just because he's cute and has a big dick he can do what he wants. But he doesn't realize he's using women, abusing them, and leaving them broken in his wake."

"He's dead."

She froze. Her eyes held unshed tears. Her chin trembled. And she sat down again. "When? How?" she said softly.

"That's what I'm trying to find out. The impression I had of him was that he was such a nice guy, but the more I learn about him, the more I realize he might have many enemies who wanted him dead."

"And you thought I killed him?"

I shrugged. "To be honest, I wasn't sure. Anything is possible."

"Well, I didn't. Wish I had though. When you find out who did it, tell me so I can shake their hand." She sat back in the chair and sighed wearily. She closed her eyes for a moment. When she opened them again, she added, "I've wished for this day for so long, and now that it's happened, I feel lost. I wish I could've seen the look on his face when it happened. I hope he suffered."

"Tell me about him," I asked, wanting to get her out of her head and to speak with me. "What did he do to you? What's his M.O.?"

After a moment she looked me in the eye, silently conveying a message I didn't understand. "We worked together at Ben's warehouse and soon became friends. He was charming, enigmatic, and people flocked to him. But... he knew this and used it to his advantage. He used it to get things from people, whether it was free drinks, meals, drugs, or sex. He used everyone. For some strange reason, he'd left me alone. We became closer friends until one night we'd been drinking after a shift, and he escorted me home to make sure I was okay. I stupidly invited him up for coffee to wake up. He offered to make the coffee. I remember nothing after that, only that the coffee had an aftertaste that reminded me of an oily plant." She shrugged. "It hit me quickly, and then I woke up the next morning naked on my bed with blood on the sheets. I thought I was dying." She shook her head. "My body was sore. I didn't know what he did to me, so I went to the hospital for tests. I'm grateful he used condoms, but still. All that blood was from him fucking me so hard and in both holes."

"I'm sorry that happened to you. Why didn't you go to the police?"

"The doctor at the hospital took some blood and found nothing. I don't know what he used to drug me. The police would've laughed in my face. I had no evidence, and he took the used condom with him. They'll say I invited him, that I wanted him in my apartment, and that I wanted to have sex. That I should've said no. I could've said no but I remember nothing about that night."

Unfortunately, this happened often. The justice system rarely supported the victim when she had the guts to come forward, but on the other side, sometimes women would wrongly accuse men. It was a slippery slope. One needed to tread lightly, and one needed evidence; I needed to get the Body Count book.

"It's obviously something the doctor didn't know to look for," I said. "Where do you think he got the stuff from?"

She shrugged. "He sold drugs. It could've been the same people who supplied him with the drugs."

I needed to speak with Lucky again and find out who could've done this.

"Do you know of any other victims?"

"None that I can think of now."

"Does Tom have any parents or siblings?"

"Nah, he said his parents died when he was a kid and went to live with his grandfather, who died a couple of years ago. And no siblings. Well, that's what he said, but he could've been lying about all that. I asked him what he did to me and he said I came on to him. He rejected me at first, but apparently I wouldn't take no for an answer. I remember he still laughed, told me I begged for his big fat dick. He made me question my reality even though I knew I'd never do that. He's a liar and no matter what he said I couldn't believe him. I just want to forget it ever happened and move on with my life."

Chapter Seventeen

DONNIE

I FINISHED my coffee and threw the cup in the trash can before heading up to the apartment. "I heard it's bloody," I said when James joined me on the stairs.

"Do we have a name for the victim yet?"

"Um," I started, checking my notebook, "Tom Westbrook."

"Is he thirty-five and a personal trainer?"

I stopped on the last step and stared down at my partner. The lines between my brows deepened. "You know him?"

"Shit," he said, stopping beside me. "Yeah, met the guy last night with Dana and her friend from yoga, Pamela."

"No way," I continued to the apartment. "You might need to excuse yourself from the case, buddy."

"I hope not. Dana and I left around twelve last night and came home. So, anything could've happened from then until now. It doesn't mean we were around."

"Let's first see what it looks like, and we can ask our captain what to do."

We slipped booties over our shoes and gloved our hands before entering. The open-plan apartment was very masculine, with leather couches, dark wood, minimal decor, no curtains, and face brick walls. It reminded me of something out of GQ magazine.

In the kitchen, there had been a struggle; a broken champagne bottle; my booties kept sticking to the floor. Along with the broken glass and dried champagne, there were drops of dried blood and with smeared blood, like someone had tried cleaning up. Someone had also broken items on the counter.

The smell of death grew stronger as we neared the bedroom. There were lab technicians working the scene already, with the coroner hovering over the body. I couldn't tell where the blood began, and the red silk sheets ended.

"What do you have for us?" James asked, standing beside me. "Looks like a mess."

"Yeah," Dr. Warryn said without looking our way. He took the liver temp. "He's been dead about eight or nine hours."

"So time of death is around two this morning," James confirmed, writing it down in his notebook.

"Looks that way." Dr. Warryn stood up and stretched out his back. Today he wore a blue bow tie to match his navy suit. He combed his salt and pepper colored hair to one side, and his brown eyes looked more tired than usual. The man was classy even though he had a porn-type-mustache. His husband loved him, and that's all that counted. "He bled to death." He pointed at the large laceration on the victim's neck. "I'll need to test the knife we found under the pillow to see if it's the murder weapon, and then I'll let you know." He pointed at a bloody spot beside the victim's pillow.

The victim was on his stomach looking to his left; his blue eyes unseeing and his sandy-blond hair matted with blood. The red silk sheets gathered around his naked waist. While the area beside him showed someone had slept there; they had either done this to the victim or had woken up to the shock of their life.

"Did you find anything else?" I asked, stepping closer.

"The team is still busy collecting traces and lifting fingerprints. I'll let you know when the results come in."

"Thanks."

"He's a big guy," Dr. Warryn added. "But he has no defensive wounds on his hands. The person who did this made sure he was fast asleep and sliced him before he woke up. I'm thinking they drugged him." He pointed at the glitter on the victim's hand along with a stamp. "He may have gone to a party and taken something either willingly or against his will. I'll test for everything just to be sure." He patted his bag. "And I'll try to do the autopsy today."

"Thanks, Doc," I said. "Let's check out the bathroom."

One technician was collecting samples from the shower drain; pulled strands of long hair out. Then they moved to the basin and did the same. There were blood drops in and around the shower and basin.

James opened the closet.

"See anything?" I asked.

"Nah," he said, closing the closet. "Bed is gruesome."

"Yeah, seems he bled out quickly."

"Hmm."

A technician assisted Dr. Warryn in putting the body in a bag and onto the gurney for transporting.

The bedside tables each had a lamp, but the one on Tom's side also had a clock, his cellphone, car keys, money, and a small empty bag. The blood had dried on the carpet, leaving it looking browner than red.

"We'll be off," Dr. Warryn said, grabbing his bags. "I'll let you know when I'm done."

"Thanks, Doc," James said. After they left, he turned to me and said, "We need to find Pam. She might've slept beside him or knows who did."

I nodded. "Yeah, I'm thinking the same. Hopefully we find her alive, and she can tell us what happened."

"We need to see if anyone remembers them from last night."

I nodded my agreement and approached her side of the bed and went down on my hands and knees to look under the bed. "There's something here," I said, calling over the officer with the camera. I got out of his way, and a technician reached for the item.

"It's lipstick," the tech said, holding it up so we could see it. "Dark cherry."

"We must get Pam's DNA," James said.

"Do you have her address?"

"Yes, it's not too far from here."

Chapter Eighteen

DANA

ELIZABETH'S COFFEE shop was across town, and I had to pass Tom's apartment to get back to Lucky's. As I neared Tom's apartment block, those familiar red and blue lights flashed; ambulance, police cruisers, along with Donnie and James's vehicle. The men were outside speaking; their conversation seemed intense. Then, as I passed them, two men dressed in white were carrying a body bag towards a van.

I contemplated stopping and speaking with James but decided against it. He'd most likely address Tom's death with me tonight when he got home, and Donnie would know that we spent the evening together with Pam and Tom. It was too coincidental to ignore. They would want to know where Pamela was, and it relieved me she'd told me nothing about what she was doing or where she'd go. I didn't want to know. I didn't want to lie to James or my brother.

I headed straight for Lucky's apartment, the squirrel on the wall taunting me as I drove up to the curb and parked the car. When I knocked on Lucky's door, it took him a while to respond.

"Yeah?" he mumbled on the other side. Something banged against the wall, followed by his cursing. He seemed to always do something before opening his front door; the first time I was here he dropped a glass.

"Lucky, it's Dana. I was here a couple of hours ago?"

The door opened. "Why are you back?" he asked, squinting with one eye, the other closed.

"Can I come inside? I have another question I need to ask."

He opened the door wider and limped towards the kitchen. I closed the door behind me and leaned against the kitchen island. He drank a glass of water and shuddered; at least now both eyes were open but red.

"Are you okay?"

"I will be. Just smoked some nasty shit, man." Another shudder. "Awful stuff. Fuck! I'm glad my face didn't fall off."

"Who supplies the drugs?"

"I ain't no rat," he said angrily.

I raised my hand. "I mean no disrespect. It's just I want to know if the person who supplies your drugs could've supplied Tom with his date rape drug because it was undetected when they tested Elizabeth's blood. Please help me figure this out."

Lucky arched both bushy eyebrows. He stepped closer, his blue/green eyes redder, and sighed. "It's possible, but I honestly don't know. Tom bought directly from Miguel and never shared with me how he went about it."

"Can Miguel make his own drugs?"

He nodded.

"What else can Miguel do?"

"He's a pharmacist at his pharmacy. I won't tell you

where it is though, can't have you or the cops busting his balls or mine." He coughed and spat into a mug on the table. I recoiled in revulsion.

"So, Miguel could've made the date rape drug for Tom?" I said. It was more of a statement than a question, but I wanted to see how Lucky responded.

"I know what you're trying to do. I'm high, not stupid; you're asking the same question differently, but I'm not falling for it. I won't give Miguel up; I already said maybe it was him."

"Are you using the drug?"

"Shit, no man, just weed. Why would you ask such a thing? Tom was on his own using that shit. And I've already told you; Tom didn't even need to use it; life messed him up enough."

"Did Tom ever disclose what the drug did?"

"It just makes them forget. Once it's in their system, they don't know what's happening around them. They can walk and talk and all that. They look fine but they can't remember any details. And yeah, the drug leaves their system after a couple of hours; it's undetectable."

"Do you know what it's called?"

"Nah, man, it's this new shit Miguel concocted. Nobody knows what's in there but him. He's a genius but a psycho. He's one guy I don't want to get on his bad side, if you know what I mean."

It relieved me Lucky had relaxed enough around me to open up about these drugs and to tell me more about Miguel. He was high and could be lying about everything, but it's a start. "What other drugs does Miguel produce and give to you to sell?" I asked.

"Ecstasy mainly; like the drugs I gave to Tom last night."

I'd forgotten about last night for a split second and was grateful I'd declined to take any of the pills. I didn't want to know what would've happened if I'd taken one, leaving poor James to figure out what was wrong with me. It felt like I'd dodged a bullet.

"Do you supply only to that club?"

"No, I give to anyone who comes to me. The warehouse, here at home. Anywhere really."

"Do you think those pills have some of the date-rape drug ingredients?"

"Nah, man, I would've had complaints if it were so."

Chapter Nineteen

DONNIE

I DROVE, and James gave me directions on where to go. Pam's house was fifteen minutes away from Tom's apartment, and the gym where he worked was between the two residences.

"Where was the warehouse you went to?"

"Downtown," James said. "The owner, Ben, repurposed one of the old factories. It looks great, since he kept most of the features. Up here," he pointed at a white picket fenced home in a safe neighborhood.

I parked the car and killed the ignition. We climbed out of the car, and traversed up the path towards the front door. Before we could knock, the door opened.

"Oh no," a man said. His eyes wide. "Is she dead?"

"Excuse me?" James said.

"My wife. I reported her missing this morning when she didn't come home last night."

"Are you Ethan?" I asked, remembering the information I found on our system.

"Yes."

"Sir," James continued, "can we come in and ask you some questions?"

Ethan opened the door wider. "Have a seat." He motioned towards the nearby couches.

"Where were you last night?" I asked, scanning the room before sitting down. On the mantelpiece were family photos, portraits adorned the walls, and there were large plants in each corner.

"I was out of town at a conference and came home when I couldn't get hold of Pam. She said she was home, but when she wasn't answering any of my calls, I cut my trip short to see where she was. I went to the police station this morning to fill in a missing person report."

"So, you don't know where she was?" I asked.

He shook his head. "Why? What's happened? Have you found her?"

"We thought she might be home," James said. "We would like to speak to her in connection with a murder—"

"Murder?" Ethan said. "What murder?"

"She was out with a gentleman found murdered this morning."

"Who?" He asked.

"Her personal trainer from the gym."

"Tom? I know Tom, but why was she out with him? Where did they go?" Ethen asked, his tone raised, and his hands fisted.

"Do you know of anyone who wanted to hurt Tom?" I asked.

"No," his brows scrunched together.

"Were you aware they were together?"

"No! I don't know what you're trying to get at, but all this is news to me." Ethan choked on the last word. "Where is Pam? Where is my wife? Did Tom do something to her, and she defended herself?"

"We're still busy investigating," James said. "Could we take some of your wife's hair to compare it with the DNA found at the scene?"

Ethan pursed his lips. "Pam couldn't have hurt anyone," he said. "Please find her?" He stood and headed for the stairs. He was gone for a while and returned with a hairbrush. James stood and opened an evidence bag, which Ethan dropped inside.

"Does Pam have another cellphone number?" I asked.

He shook his head. "Just the one. What will I tell our children? They'll be home tomorrow."

"WHAT DO YOU THINK?" I asked as I turned the key, and the engine roared to life.

"Not sure. He's a hard one to read. I'm going to check his alibi for last night," James said, making notes in the folder.

"Okay."

"Should we check out the gym?"

"Yes," I said, merging with traffic.

The gym was full of sweaty people either running on the spot or trying to lift the heaviest weights possible. We asked to speak with the manager, who was yet to arrive in his office.

"When should—" I started saying when the manager walked in. I'd ask James after the interview about whether we should speak to our captain about his connection to the deceased.

"Sorry to keep you waiting," Scott Craddock said, sitting behind his desk. He had the reddest curly hair I'd ever seen before, a freckled nose, and green eyes. His muscles strained against the top he wore, and although he seemed intimidating, he was probably a softy underneath that hard exterior.

"We'd like to ask you a few questions about Tom Westbrook," I said, opening my notebook.

"Tom? Why? What's he done now?" Scott said, chuckling.

"We're investigating his murder," James said.

Scott sat up straight, and cleared his throat. "Shit, really? Jeez, man, you could've started with that. What happened?"

"That's what we're trying to figure out," James continued. "What was he like as an employee?"

"Fine? I mean, he's had a few complaints—"

"About?" I asked.

"Not showing up on time. He seemed out of it. Um," Scott thought, "inappropriate touching that was excused because he was trying to help the woman up off the floor. Nothing was serious enough to fire him, though. And I went through HR."

"Could we have copies of those records?" I asked.

"Sure," Scott said, making a note.

"Do you know anyone who would want to hurt him?" James asked.

"No," Scott said, shaking his head. "I mean, he had one altercation with another guy about a month ago. He's got short, curly black hair, a thick red beard, and bushy eyebrows. If I had to guess, he was a drug user," he shrugged, "I don't know what they were arguing about, but neither seemed happy."

"Did you see that guy here before?"

"Never and didn't see him again. I remember it only because it was recent and a crowd of our clients gathered around them. We all thought they were going to fight."

"I don't suppose you got the guy's name?" I asked.

"No, sorry."

"Did any of your cameras pick this up?"

"No, it happened in the parking lot."

"Hey boss," a man said, poking his head through the open door. "That lady is back demanding to speak with you."

"Okay, take her to the conference room and offer her some coffee. I'll be right out," he said to his employee. "Anything else, or can I tend to that fire?" He thumbed at the door.

"Can you think of anything that happened you'd consider out of the ordinary?" I asked. "The people he trained, someone looking for him, anything at all?"

"No, not at the moment."

"Here's my card if you think of anything else," James said, handing it to him.

"Any luck with Pam's number?" I asked when we were on the road again.

"Straight to voicemail."

"Okay."

"What about the warehouse?" James asked, glancing at his watch.

"There's no urgency. Let's hold off until tomorrow. It's getting late, and I promised Maddy I'd be home in time for dinner tonight."

Chapter Twenty

DANA

I LEFT Lucky so he could soothe the headache that was bothering him and decided it was enough for today. I didn't want to ask questions about Tom at the gym because I was sure Donnie and James would start there, so I headed home.

I researched the five names Lucky had given me, coming up with nothing. I was sure I'd copied the names and numbers correctly from Lucky's phone, unless he'd entered them incorrectly. Not wanting to waste any more time on it, I poured a glass of red wine and started making spaghetti Bolognese. It was after seven by the time I switched off the stove and dished up the food when the front door opened and closed.

"Hey, I'm in the kitchen," I said, carrying our plates to the dining room table.

"Smells delicious," James said with a grin. He closed the gap and kissed my cheek. "How was your day?"

"Good, productive. Glad it's still the weekend." I sat down and waited for him to join me.

He dropped his bag on the kitchen counter and left his gun and badge in the drawer near the dining table.

"How was your day?" I asked as he sat down.

"Uhm, I need to tell you something," he said, not happy. "Your friend Pam, do you know where she is?" He played with his knife and fork, not looking at me.

"No idea, why? What's wrong?"

"It's about the guy she was with last night, Tom; someone murdered him."

I couldn't act to save my life, but I knew I had to be surprised upon hearing the news. "What? What do you mean, murdered? When? How? You don't think Pam…" I said, leaving my sentence hanging.

"We're still investigating and don't know if it's her, but we'd like to speak to her and find out when she last saw him. You and I left the club close to midnight, and they were still there. We're placing his time of death at around two in the morning. Whoever did this might have hurt Pam, but so far, we haven't heard of a body matching her description showing up anywhere."

"Do you know how they killed him?"

"Dr. Warryn is busy with the autopsy as we speak, but based on what we saw, they cut his carotid artery."

"That's terrible," I said, glancing at our food. "Eat before it gets cold," I said, forking some into my mouth. "Do you have any thoughts about what might have happened?"

"Tom is a big guy and can't be easily overpowered," James said while chewing. "Which makes me think someone drugged and then killed him."

"It makes sense," I said. Tom was tall and strong; he was a personal trainer and worked out often. And based on what others had said about him, he was used to taking drugs, and it didn't affect him as much as it would Pam.

We ate in silence, and I didn't know what else to ask. Lying didn't come naturally to me, and James would know, so I thought best not to ask any more questions unless James offered information.

"I found the crime scene strange," he finally said, finishing his food.

"Oh yeah? Why's that?" A sinking feeling in my gut told me James had discovered something I'd left behind, or he'd found evidence confirming Pam killed Tom.

"The scene felt staged, or rather, some parts felt like it might have been. For example, they cleaned the knife and placed it under the pillow, but then they left hair in the shower. It made little sense, like the person who did it didn't know what they were doing."

"Yeah, that is strange." That's when Pam cleaned her prints off it and placed the knife back. I'd forgotten she'd showered; I should've told her to remove her hair.

"Then in the kitchen it looked like a struggle had taken place, and we found two different blood splatters, so either two people cut themselves or one person cut themself twice. Someone else was there. What bothers me about that is why didn't they clean that area if they struggled with Tom in the kitchen. They had cleaned some parts, others, not. Same with the shower, that was wiped down, yet they left the hair." He shook his head and leaned against the chair back.

"Yeah, it makes no sense."

"Anyway, what's for dessert?" he asked with a sly grin.

I laughed. "I'm almost done eating. We're having a hot pudding, though. Something sweet and sticky with ice cream."

"Take your time," he said, squeezing my hand gently. "All I've done was speak about my day. How was yours?"

"It was good," I said, finishing the last bite. "A client paid, and I started a new case. For now, it's just research and interviews. I'll continue again on Monday."

"I need to work tomorrow," he said, sounding deflated. "I know we're supposed to go to your folks for Sunday lunch, but Donnie and I need to speak to someone at the warehouse we went to on Friday. It was too late to go now." He rubbed his face and yawned.

"Don't worry about it," I said, reaching for his hand. "Let me know if I can help."

"The number I had for Pam goes straight to her voice-mail. If she reaches out to you, will you call me?"

"Sure," I said, standing. "Dessert?"

"Absolutely."

Chapter Twenty-One

PAM

THE ONLY SAFE place I thought of where I could go was my mother's empty house in Oak Brook. It's just a quick twenty-five-minute drive from Chicago, and she wouldn't be home for a month. She was on a cruise ship somewhere off the coast of Europe with her latest boyfriend, twenty years her junior. I didn't mind as long as he wasn't using my mom for her money.

"Thanks," I said, handing the cab driver cash. I'd withdrawn all the money from my bank account, which should keep me afloat for a while if all I bought was food. I didn't have enough money to travel far unless it's an emergency. I still needed cash to get back to Chicago.

I traversed up the footpath towards the front door, grateful it was a quiet neighborhood with no nosy neighbors. Glancing around and seeing nobody watching me, I picked up the fake white rock and opened the bottom to get the spare key. I opened the front door, switched off the alarm and locked the door behind me.

Leaning against the door, I closed my eyes and breathed

deeply. I smiled; Mom's house smelled like her; her perfume was floral and distinctive. I'd smelled nothing similar on anyone else before; only her. With a weary sigh, I pushed away from the door and headed for my room upstairs. After all these years, Mom had kept my room as I'd left it, making me smile.

I walked past a mirror in the hallway and stopped; I was pale and my face gaunt. My light brown eyes were darker than usual and puffy. Even my brown hair seemed black, but it could just be the lighting, or I needed a good, long shower, maybe some food and lots of water.

I threw my bag onto my bed and entered the ensuite bathroom. I cringed when I saw myself again; the clothing I'd taken from Tom's place left me feeling uncomfortable, and I undressed quickly. Staring at the crumpled clothing on the floor all I saw was Tom's lifeless body covered in blood; and his red sheets covered in blood. Visions of my body and fingers dripping with his blood. There was so much of his warm blood everywhere.

I shivered as memories of this morning flashed before me; Tom's cold body covered in dried, warm, and wet blood; it was a grisly scene I'd never experienced before in all my forty-two years on earth. How anybody working jobs who saw that regularly stayed sane was beyond me?

I couldn't understand what had happened or why the knife was under my pillow. But what bothered me the most was why I couldn't remember. If I did this, why couldn't I remember anything? I probably should've gone to the hospital to have blood taken, but I couldn't risk it now. Dana's husband and brother could be on the case already and looking for me.

Heading for the shower, I glimpsed the bruises and scratches on my back and arms in the mirror. I stopped and stared, remembering how rough Ethan had been. But the bruises? Where did the bruises come from? Perhaps Tom was also rough last night. I wished I remembered.

Swallowing the lump in my throat, I turned the shower taps on and waited for the water to heat. Waves of goose-bumps spread across my skin the moment I touched the warm water. It felt heavenly as I forgot about the last twenty-four hours. My mind was clearer, and I could think, but all that came crashing down when flashes of all that red hit me like a ton of bricks, and I cried. I crumpled to the shower floor and sobbed until my head hurt. Tom was dead. Someone had murdered him while I was next to him, yet they didn't hurt me. *Why?*

Thoughts of Tom being involved in something illegal came to mind, or someone was vindictive. *What did Tom do?*

I started shivering, my teeth chattering. The water was chilly. I'd lost time sitting on the shower floor deep in thought. Switching off the taps, I reached for a towel, huddling in the fabric's warmth, wishing my mother was here to hold me. I was forty-two and still craved my mother's hugs; there was nothing better. She could always fix my boo-boos; I knew she couldn't fix this one, but I still wanted her comforting hug.

This was what happened to women who cheated on their husbands; except karma found me quickly, leaving a dead man beside me.

Opening my closet, the old clothing smelled like dust, so I went to Mom's room instead. We had similar-sized bodies, and her clothing would be in better condition. I needed to buy new underwear and would do so once dressed. I also needed food if I were to stay here for a few days. And I needed a burner phone. I couldn't remember what else I needed to get; hopefully, I'd remember at the store.

The market was within walking distance of Mom's house. When I reached the building, I hesitated at first, thinking the automatic doors wouldn't open for me, but they did on the first try. Relieved I didn't have to wave at the sensor and draw attention to myself, I entered the store and reached for a trolley. Glancing nervously around to see who recognized me, but there were only two other customers, and neither of them noticed me. I didn't think I was on the news yet. I exhaled a shaky breath and filled the trolley with food and new underwear.

I didn't want to stay outside for long. The last thing I needed was to see a picture of my face in the newspaper and then come face to face with someone looking at the same paper and staring at me. I paid for my items and hurried home.

I unpacked the food in the pantry and fridge, then slipped on fresh underwear. Once I had a full glass of wine, I sat on the sofa and stared outside at the birds and trees and everything that wasn't my life. I didn't want to think about what was happening right now, about ruining my life, my marriage, and losing my children.

The moment I thought of my kids, I downed the glass of wine and cried. It was too late; I'd already ruined everything. Perhaps the best thing for me to do was to end things; to end myself. It wouldn't help solve what really happened, but right now everything pointed to me as the guilty person. Everything felt hopeless right now.

Before trashing my cellphone, I'd saved the photos I took of Tom's apartment to the cloud, but I didn't want to look at them again; it was too fresh, too raw, too bloody. I should log into the cloud and delete them all, but I didn't want to yet.

I wondered whether Dana had spoken with anyone

about Tom or if she'd discovered anything that would prove my innocence. I needed to know what was going on back home or I'd drive myself crazy. Dana was the only person I could reach out to, and I hoped she was still in my corner. If I ever wanted to see my kids, I needed Dana now more than ever.

"It's me," I messaged. "How are things going?"

"Hey girlfriend," Dana responded, trying to sound upbeat. *"Still figuring out. Lie low. Stay calm. We'll get to the bottom of it."*

"Thank you."

I appreciated her helping me; I knew she was good at her job. I hoped she could solve this before her brother arrested me.

Chapter Twenty-Two

DANA

I FIRST NEEDED to research Miguel. I wanted to find out who this person was and if he was safe to approach; probably not, but I still needed information on him. There had to be something online I could find and perhaps locate his pharmacy. I no longer had a hacker friend who could do special in-depth searches for me, so I had to rely on what's available on the internet.

I searched for *Miguel Pharmacy* and found only one option in the Chicago area. His pharmacy was also near Lucky's apartment. Now I needed more information about who Miguel was.

After a couple of hours, I had enough information about Miguel I'd found on social media. He'd been married once. They had a son, Miguel Jr., who'd passed away soon after birth. Then his wife had died of cancer, and if I cross-referenced the timelines, it was around the same time Tom and Lucky started dealing. Miguel probably needed an outlet for his grief; it was the worst possible outlet. He'd gone through many tragedies, and I felt sorry for him, but that didn't excuse his making illegal party drugs along with a date-rape drug.

I'd first scope out Miguel's pharmacy before going to Tom's apartment to search for the Body Count book. I didn't think there would be any police presence at the apartment, but I'd be cautious just in case.

Miguel's pharmacy was called *Big M's Pharmacy*. I parked across the street from his pharmacy and watched. It was a busy area, and his shop always had clients coming in and out. There were four other employees, but Miguel was the only pharmacist.

I took a few pictures and then realized nothing much was happening. I wanted to follow Miguel to his home or the place where he made the drugs so that I could send Donnie and James an anonymous tip.

I merged with traffic and headed to Tom's apartment. It was quiet. There were no policemen anywhere near the building. I slipped on some disposable gloves, entered the apartment building from the back entrance and used the stairs. The first time I was here with Pam, I checked all areas and was grateful there were no cameras. But I didn't want to use the front entrance in case the police arrived; I knew almost all of them at the precinct, and they'd tell James and Donnie I was here.

Police tape crisscrossed the locked apartment door. I picked the door lock and opened it, climbing between the police tape without disturbing it, and carefully closed the door behind me.

Scanning the open-plan living room, I saw the bookcase against the wall near a second television. I checked all the books in search of the Body Count book but found nothing. Then I felt under each shelf for a secret compartment, touching something on the bottom shelf that might be it.

Getting down onto my hands and knees to get a better look, there it was, a book sitting in a metal frame. I needed to get all the way inside and pulled the book towards the wall to get it out.

I sat down with the book on my lap and paged through it; the first page was a picture of Tom and a very young naked girl. She was completely out of it. They were sitting on the bed; he had one arm around her as if keeping her upright, and his other was holding her hand, gripping his naked penis. Her hair was messy, her dark lipstick had smudged across her left cheek, and her eyeliner gave her dark rings under her eyes. He was maybe ten or twelve years younger, had the biggest grin, and underneath the photo he'd written;

"Miguel's latest product works like a charm. Crushed this girl without trying. Now to see the aftereffects."

I wanted to throw up.

On the next page, a girl's legs hung over the edge of the bed with her pants around her ankles, her ass in the air, with blood between her legs. And underneath he'd written;

"Stacy wanted to try some anal. Nailed that tight ass over and over."

On and on it went. Pictures of docile women in various stages of nakedness and Tom's cruel words underneath. I paged through to the last entry, and there was Pam. She was naked, spread-eagled on his bed. Those red silk sheets bunched in various places, obvious they'd already slept together. What surprised me was the words he wrote beneath;

"I've found someone worth my while. She calms my demons. She makes me whole. I want to be a better man because of her, yet I find myself taking her picture like the others. I want her (need her) to be my

last, my everything, and my forever; I want her, and only her until I die."

The rest of the pages were blank, but I checked anyway. Right at the back, on the last page, was a picture of Tom snuggling Pam; both asleep. I saw no blood; someone had taken this picture before they cut his throat. It also meant that Pam was asleep and couldn't have hurt Tom. They'd drugged her, and she'd slept until the next morning. In this photo, Tom was just asleep.

Who took the Polaroid picture?

———

NEEDING to show this to James, but I couldn't. I didn't want to answer his questions about how I'd come about it. I didn't want to lie to my husband, but he needed to see this Body Count book. It was disturbing, to say the least, but it would assist Pam in proving her innocence. Obviously, someone else was there with them that night, and they knew about the book. They knew about the drugs, and the only person I could think of was Lucky, but if it was him, why did he tell me about it. It would lead me straight to him, so I doubted it was him.

I couldn't think of anyone else other than it being a woman Tom had hurt and put in his book. I took pictures of all the pages of the book and placed the book back in its metal frame under the bottom shelf. The only way Donnie and James would find out about this book was if Lucky told them or I phoned in an anonymous tip.

Standing, I surveyed the apartment. The bed had its bedding removed, leaving behind red stains on the mattress. The living area had minimal damage, while the kitchen still had the smaller broken pieces of the champagne bottle scattered everywhere.

I couldn't stay here much longer and hurried outside. Once in my car, I headed back to Miguel's pharmacy. I parked and felt deflated. The doors were closed, and the lights were off. It was already two in the afternoon on a Sunday, so Miguel most likely closed early over the weekend.

I locked my car with the key fob and crossed the street. The operating times on the window revealed what I'd already thought, and he'd probably gone home already, but when something caught my eye at the back, I ducked to one side. Slowly, I moved forward to get a better look through the window, and there he was in the back packing medication into white bags.

I traversed the alley between the pharmacy and the store next door, entering the parking area behind the pharmacy. There was only one vehicle parked nearest the backdoor to the pharmacy. I took a picture, ensuring I could see the registration number, and headed back to my vehicle.

I waited until the blue Ford pickup drove past, ensuring at least two cars were between us before I followed him. After twenty minutes, he parked at a residential home that had a sizable piece of land. I parked a short distance away and watched.

Miguel exited his vehicle and entered the house. A short time later he crossed the yard and entered a shed towards the left-hand side of the property. I climbed out of my vehicle and approached the main gate. Glancing around the neighborhood, but there was nobody in sight. I scaled over the gate and landed in a crouching position and stuck to the fence as I approached the shed.

The shed was small, yet as I neared the open window, I saw a hole in the floor and stairs going down into a hidden room below. I needed to get a better look at what's down there. Using my phone, I took a few pictures. I pocketed my phone and turned around and stopped before hitting his chest.

"What are you doing in my yard?" Miguel asked, his tone filled with violence.

And for the first time in a long time, I had no words.

Chapter Twenty-Three

DONNIE

"ETHAN'S ALIBI CHECKED OUT," James said as we neared the warehouse. "He was at a conference, then came straight home Saturday morning when he couldn't reach Pam." James read from his notes, then pocketed the book. "And now for this place."

"I didn't know it existed," I said, stepping into the unknown warehouse that doubled as a nightclub every Friday night.

"It looks different during the day," James said, following me into the dark entrance.

"Are you the cops who called?" A bald man with beady brown eyes said, approaching with something in his hands.

"Is that a weapon?" I asked, squinting and reached for my gun.

"No, it's posters," he said, holding it up in the light and unravelling them. "Don't shoot. They're just posters," he said, lowering them. "I'm Ben." He proffered a hand.

"I'm Detective Mulder and he's Detective Michaels," I said, holstering my weapon.

"Is this regarding Tom?"

"Yeah, how do you know?"

"A lady P.I. was here asking about him, so I figured you're here for that too."

James and I shared a knowing look. It could only be Dana sticking her nose where it didn't belong.

"What did you tell her?" James asked.

"Told her Tom used to sell drugs with his friend Lucky, and that Tom may have drugged women."

James had shared with me that Tom and Pamela had taken ecstasy Friday night, but now we're discovering he had ulterior motives. "Tell us more about his drugging women."

"Just that he'd drug them and take them home, you know, and do awful things to them."

I shook my head.

"I also gave the private investigator the details of an ex-employee who I think Tom may have hurt."

"Can you give us her details and where to find her."

"Yeah, sure, one moment." Ben went to his office and returned shortly with the information scribbled on a piece of paper. "Not sure if Lucky still lives in that apartment with the squirrel painted on the side, but he must because that P.I. girl didn't return asking for more information."

"Thanks."

"What happened to Tom? The P.I. said nothing other than wanting to understand who Tom was."

"Someone murdered him," James said.

Ben's mouth dropped open, then he quickly schooled his features. "Damn, I didn't know. Do you think it's drug-related?"

"Not sure; that's what we need to find out," I said.

"I see, damn, I can't believe it. I mean, I could see

someone wanting to kill the bastard, but still. Knowing it happened hits differently, you know."

"What do you think?" James asked when we were back in the car.

"Things have shifted away from Pam," I said. "We need to dig deeper into Tom; from the sounds of it, he wasn't such a great guy. It's possible that a woman he'd hurt finally took her revenge out on him, or his druggy friend Lucky may have something to do with it."

"I wouldn't have thought that," James said. "When I met him on Friday, he had this good energy surrounding him, like life was excellent, and he treated everyone right." He shook his head. "I wouldn't have thought he needed to drug women to have sex. The guy was handsome. He could get any girl he wanted."

"We need to find out more about Lucky, Elizabeth Marconi, and Tom. Where he's from? Who his family is? That kind of thing."

We arrived at the apartment building with a squirrel painted on the side and headed for Lucky's apartment. We knocked a few times, but when we heard no sound on the other side, we went back to the car.

The coffee shop where Elizabeth worked was closed on Sunday's and we had no other details for her home address.

"I guess we're heading back to the station," James said.

"Yeah, let's do some research. We can chat to them tomorrow."

James investigated Elizabeth while I checked out Lucky. I searched for all known drug dealers with that name in the Chicago area, and there was only one, and he lived at the address we went to. Police had arrested Lucky four times for possession of narcotics. Reading the notes on file, he went to the same school as Tom; both were the same age. If I had to guess, they'd been friends since school and continued selling drugs after school. The only difference now Lucky still dealt in drugs while Tom became a personal trainer.

It saddened me how a person's facial features changed as they aged when they took illegal drugs regularly. Lucky's face went from young and fresh to aging him ten years older than he was. The mugshot from his arrest last year showed he had more wrinkles around his eyes and mouth, and his face was gaunt even with the beard, like life had smacked him in the face a few times. I doubted he'd live to see his fifties if he continued using.

I opened Tom's file; he'd been arrested three times. He'd lived with his uncle from when he was a teenager. His uncle had died mysteriously in his sleep on Tom's eighteenth birthday. The uncle had a long list of charges against him, which included sexual assault of a minor.

"Hey," James said, knocking on my desk. "Find anything?"

"I think Tom's first kill was his uncle."

"Yeah?"

"Hmm, and it's possible the uncle molested Tom from the time he moved in. His mom passed away when he was sixteen, but no mention of his dad living with them. The only living relative was this asshole uncle." I shook my head. "He would've had better luck in the system."

"Tom probably developed mental health issues from his teenage years," James sat across from me. "Anyway," he raised a folder in his hand, "Elizabeth Marconi was in hospital two years ago where they collected evidence following a rape."

I arched both eyebrows and leaned back in my chair. "Do we know if the hospital's pathology lab kept it?"

He nodded.

"We need to send that over to our forensics."

"Already done. I'm telling you now, it's Tom's if we're to believe Ben." James turned the page.

"Why didn't they arrest Tom?"

"She didn't file any charges. I don't think she wanted to go through all the hoops necessary for a conviction."

I shook my head. Sometimes the system rewarded the wrong people. "Did you find anything else?"

"Nah, we could always go to her apartment. I have the address now."

I glanced at my watch. "We should first make sure you can stay on the case."

"Already asked, and the captain said it's fine."

"Okay, let's go to Elizabeth's home and then see if Lucky is back."

―――――

WE KNOCKED on Elizabeth's apartment door, but nobody answered. As we turned to leave, a woman I recognized approached. She had a unique look; her short blue/black hair, white eyebrows, striking blue eyes, and frail-looking body was hard to miss.

"Miss Marconi?" James asked, standing to one side so she could reach her door.

"Yeah?" she said, glancing nervously at us.

"I'm Detective Michaels, and that's Detective Mulder. We'd like to speak with you regarding Tom Westbrook."

"What do you want to know?" she asked, standing with her back against her door and folding her arms across her chest.

"What kind of relationship did you have with Tom?" James continued with the interview questions.

"We were work colleagues."

"Nothing else?"

"What are you getting at?" The lines between her eyes deepened.

"Do you have any reason to kill him?" James asked. "Someone murdered him on Saturday morning."

She stared deadpan. She didn't even blink. "It's true then," she finally said. "When that private investigator showed up telling me someone had murdered him, I was skeptical at first, but now, I'm glad he's gone."

I couldn't believe Dana had already spoken with her; when I saw my sister again, I'd give her a piece of my mind. James flinched; I think it bothered him too that Dana was interviewing our suspects before we did. Dana was messing with our case.

"Yeah?" James said, recovering quickly. "Why's that?"

"Because he's scum. He deserved a far worse fate than death. I wish he'd suffered."

"What did he do to you?" I asked.

Elizabeth paused for a moment; then she explained how she thought they were good friends and had dismissed the rumors about him until one night they were drinking at work. He offered to escort her home safely, and she mistakenly invited him up for coffee which he made for them. She woke up the next morning naked in her bed with no recollection of the night before. He made it out how great she was and that she shouldn't worry; he didn't hurt her even though her body was sore. She went to hospital but then decided against taking it further when they found nothing in her blood. It was then that she confirmed the rumors of Tom preying on women, drugging them, having sex, and then taking pictures of them.

"Do you know how many women he's done this to?"

"At least a hundred, maybe two." She shrugged. "He'd been doing it since his twenties."

James and I shared a knowing glance. This guy made me sick; the unnecessary trauma he'd caused for all these women, and any of them could've killed him. This made our job harder because we knew nothing about the women or how we could reach any of them.

"Tom was a fun guy who loved to party," she continued. "He had good energy, you know; almost addictive. Before I knew these awful things about him, I loved being around him. But there's something so dark within him I don't think he knew what to do with it. Whatever happened to him as a kid ruined him as an adult, and I guess when someone gets badly hurt, they want to hurt others back; to share their hurt, hoping it helped. But the more he did it, the more he needed to do it. I don't know; that's just what I think. I'm sure there are lots of psychological reasons behind this that you guys could look into."

Tom had many layers to his character, and none of them were great. Everything about him made my skin crawl.

"Before we go, where were you last Friday and Saturday?" I asked. I didn't think she did it, but I still needed to check her alibi.

"Worked at the coffee shop from eight in the morning until five in the afternoon on both days. On Friday evening I went out for drinks with friends at a place called *The Gym*; it's around the corner here," she motioned with her hand, "they walked me home around two in the morning. They were too drunk to drive, so they stayed over." She pulled out her cellphone. "Here's their numbers; Tasha and Noel."

"Thanks," James said while writing their numbers down. "Last question. Did you know any of Tom's victims?"

She thought for a moment. "At first, I said no to the private investigator, but the more I thought about it, I knew one victim. She used to come to the warehouse often, and we spoke a lot at the bar while she ordered her drinks. She was a delightful girl. I bumped into her at the grocery store about a year after she'd stopped coming to the warehouse, and she'd gained so much weight; I hardly recognized her. When I touched her arm to catch her attention, she flinched. When I saw all the trauma in her eyes, I suspected something might have happened just by looking at her."

"Her name?"

"Bev Newman. It used to be Chambers. She told me she married some old guy who was very kind to her."

"Did you ask her if anything had happened between her and Tom?"

"Nah, man, she looked like a frightened bird when I saw her; jumped every time I moved. The last thing I wanted to do was bring up a traumatic event for her. Sometimes it's best to just leave things be, you know."

Chapter Twenty-Four

DANA

"YEAH, you better come quickly before I take out the garbage," Miguel said into the receiver while staring hard at me. He ended the call and leaned against the kitchen counter. "You can be glad Lucky knows you and is on his way."

Miguel was close to turning sixty, yet his physique was closer to a man in his late forties; fit and healthy. Even his brown hair was still brown. His intelligent eyes were dark brown, but it was the hard lines on his face that made him look sixty; the worry lines, lines caused by grief and stress. His voice was deep, and he spoke with a slight Hispanic accent.

I sighed wearily, mentally kicking myself for getting caught. While Miguel checked something on his phone, I took in my surroundings. The dirty yellow kitchen was old, taking me back to the sixties. It looked like he hadn't cleaned the counters in a while, and there were loads of dirty dishes in the sink. Narrowing my eyes, I noticed old photos on the walls in the next room; they looked like kids playing in a park.

Miguel cleared his throat, catching my attention.

"Sorry for entering your yard," I said. "If you tell me what I need to know then I'll get out of your hair, and nobody has to know about this." I motioned towards my restraints. "I'm a private investigator." I shifted in my seat, the rope biting into my wrists and ankles. The chair creaked beneath my weight. "Please," I pleaded, "you don't want this on your plate right now, not when I tell you what I'm investigating."

"What information do you want?"

"About what you do in that hidden room in your shed."

He shook his head.

"Tom is dead," I said.

Miguel arched both eyebrows.

"And I think someone is framing my friend for his death. I need to understand what happened on Friday night or early Saturday morning."

"How was Tom killed?"

"His throat was slit in his sleep."

"He would've woken up. He was a light sleeper. There's no way he'd just take it. Someone drugged him."

"That's what I'm thinking, too, and I'm sure the cops know that. I also know the woman he was with would hurt no one. It's got to be someone else."

"I wonder if it's the same girl he told me about."

"Which girl?"

"Just he'd fallen for a woman at the gym. Said he'd change everything for her."

I found it interesting that Tom shared so much of his personal life with Miguel, and that he'd mentioned how he'd felt about Pam. "Hadn't he already been changing?" I asked.

"Yeah, sure, I mean he stopped dealing one or two years ago, but he didn't stop drugging women."

I hated hearing that someone did that to women. It was awful. The thing that bothered me the most was that other people knew about this and did nothing to stop Tom or warn the women; they actually encouraged it by producing more of the drug or by remaining his friend. Anyone who knew what Tom did was just as guilty for allowing it to continue.

"Did you create the drug for him? What's in it?" I asked, needing to understand more about what Miguel did. "I need to see if Tom has the same drug in his system. That way we can narrow down where the drug came from."

His smile stretched his face in two. "Rohypnol and gamma-hydroxybutyrate; otherwise known as GHB. It's a central nervous system depressant. I added just enough for the women not to remember what happened yet functional enough to answer, and then I added a herbal oil for an additional kick." He winked, raising his head as if it were a proud moment. And I wondered whether making these drugs made him feel godlike and boosted his ego.

I pulled on my restraints, wishing I could smack the maker of this awful drug across his face. "Why do it?" I asked.

"Tom became a son to me after my kid and wife died. And he asked for it," he said, raising a shoulder.

"He's a handsome man. He could have any woman he wanted. Did he say why he needed it?"

"You must understand where Tom came from and what happened to him. He has a dark side that scared him, and he couldn't deny it any longer. His uncle molested him when he was a kid, and that messed him up. Then, his father abandoned him when he was five years old, and his mom passed away when he turned sixteen. The same uncle who molested him took him in and continued hurting him. There are monsters out there—"

"That doesn't mean it gave him the right to hurt others, scar others, and traumatize all those women. It's unnecessary. It's cruel. He's left victims in his wake."

"Like I said, it's something he had to do to quieten the darkness within. I'm not condoning any of it; I'm explaining his perspective." He rubbed his face. "I had to make the drug for Tom. He threatened me; said if I didn't make it for him, he'd ensure the cops caught on to my other job. Tom was a bad guy no matter what his package looked like or how friendly he was. In the end he deceived us all."

I understood why Miguel thought that way because I thought it too. Tom was smooth, and I was sure he used his charm to disarm people, confusing them, and getting out of them what he wanted. The world was full of scumbags.

"Do you have any idea who wanted him dead?"

"I can give you a few names," he said nonchalantly.

"Well, I'd love to write them down." I moved my tied limbs.

He smirked and pushed away from the counter. He grabbed a large, sharp knife and cut the rope, freeing my hands and legs. "Don't make me regret this."

"Wait!" Lucky yelled, entering the kitchen. "Don't kill her." He stood between me and Miguel.

"Relax, Lucky," Miguel said, setting the knife down on the counter. "I'm not gonna kill her. I'm a pharmacist; I'm not in the business of killing people no matter how badly they piss me off. Besides, she needs to write things down." He winked wickedly at me.

Miguel made us coffee and continued his theory of all the people who might want to hurt Tom. There were ten names on the list who were possibilities. The problem was he didn't know where I could find them. They were just first names and no pictures; I'd only end up chasing my tail because it was too little information to go on.

Although I had nothing much to research, I at least made another *friend*; or rather, a friendly-acquaintance. The important part was that he wouldn't kill me. I thanked Miguel for the information, names, and coffee. His creepy smile was his response, but I did notice the twinkle in his eye as his dark gaze raked up and down my body. I felt violated but wouldn't voice my concern to either of them. The best thing for me was to get out of there quickly and quietly.

"Where can I drop you off?" I asked Lucky when he climbed into my car.

"My apartment, please."

I merged into traffic. It was early afternoon, and I needed to get home. I'd already missed the usual family Sunday lunch, and I wanted to make a nice dinner for James and me. And to say thanks for saving me, I offered to give Lucky a lift home.

"That could've ended differently," he said, staring out of the window. He scratched at his red beard.

"I know," I said, relieved I had walked out of there instead of leaving in a body bag. I couldn't wait to be held by James later as I counted my blessings.

"You can be glad you're charming in an annoying way," he smirked, highlighting his boyish features. Lucky was in his mid-thirties and, when he wasn't high, was quite pleasant to be around and talk with.

"Thank goodness for that," I said jokingly. "Do you know any of the people Miguel mentioned?"

"Nah, man, never heard of them. I also didn't know he and Tom were so close." He shook his head. "Just shows what I thought I knew, hey. People wear different masks depending on who they're with. I thought I knew Tom, but I obviously know nothing about him."

"You knew enough. I found the Body Count book, and to say how disgusted I am is an understatement."

"Yeah, it's sick. He showed it to me a couple of times, bragging about how he'd fucked all those girls. He was sick. Why couldn't he just bust a nut like the rest of us?"

I assumed he meant masturbation, and as much as I wanted to clarify, I didn't want to get into specifics about that topic with him. "Thank you for telling me about it. It will help my client's case," I said instead.

"Will you tell the cops about it?"

I nodded. "Definitely, they need to look closer into them and into Tom. Maybe they can find more of his victims."

"Are you any closer to finding out what happened to him?" Lucky asked with concern in his tone as he stared out of the window.

"Not sure. I'll need to follow up on a few things, but I know more today than I did yesterday." I didn't think I could get information on Tom's autopsy without arousing suspicion.

We passed a coffee shop, and I stopped. I hadn't eaten all day and didn't think Lucky had either. "Are you hungry?"

He nodded. "Famished."

We ordered burgers and milkshakes, reminding me of when I was a teenager. We sat near the window, ate in silence, and watched the people outside. Lucky frowned as he stared at a couple crossing the street.

"What's wrong?" I said, reaching over and rubbing the deep lines between his bushy eyebrows.

"I recognize that couple but can't remember from where," he said, jerking his chin at them.

"Maybe you sold them drugs?" I said nonchalantly, eating a fry.

"You know what, I think you're right. Friday night before I gave Tom his, that guy was so eager to get the special pills Miguel made, I thought he was going to hit me." He shook his head. "He was desperate to get them. Anyway, I've encountered many people like him, but I definitely remember him from Friday."

"Do you mean the spiked pills?" I asked, confirming. "The ones Miguel made specifically for Tom?"

"Yeah, I completely forgot about that," he said, shrugging.

I sighed inwardly, reining in my frustration. *What else had he forgotten to tell me?* One thing I'd realized about drug users who were also dealers, they forgot a lot of things or their stories changed mid-sentence. It's just who they'd become.

"I don't know how he knew about them, but he wanted Tom's pills. I charged him double, and he was happy to pay."

"And you carry those pills on you in case others want to buy?"

"That guy pre-ordered them. He got my phone number from somewhere and called, saying he would fetch them from me at the warehouse. Yeah, it's him. I could never forget that face."

I raised my cellphone and took a few shots of him with the blonde he was with. When I enlarged the picture, I recognized the woman.

I'D JUST FINISHED MAKING dinner when James came home. "I'm so glad I'm on time." He grinned and then kissed my temple. "Food smells delicious. How was your day?" He placed his weapon and badge on the kitchen counter and sat at the dining table.

"It was good. Did some research on a new case and learned a few new things. How was your day?" I asked, sitting beside him.

"Tell me more about your case."

"I'm just helping a friend of mine."

James looked at me as if he wanted to say something but thought against it.

After our meal, we drank tea at the table. Throughout dinner, I wanted to ask how the case was going but stopped myself a few times. But now I'd reached a point where I had to know for Pam's sake.

"Are you getting close to finding Tom's killer?"

"We're still investigating." He finished his tea and sighed. "Do you know where Pam is?" He asked, staring at me as if I knew something. "Is this the friend you're doing something for?" He arched an eyebrow.

Dammit. He had me there. I didn't want to lie to him, but I needed to protect her.

"Dana." The way he said my name left me feeling nervous. "We've spoken with Ben and Elizabeth Marconi, and both mentioned a private investigator. We know it's you."

Dammit. I couldn't lie to my husband; it wasn't worth it. Pam was my friend, but my husband came first, and I needed to respect our marriage; I needed to respect him.

"I honestly don't know where she is; all I know is she's innocent." I bit my lip thinking about the Body Count book.

"Your brother and I aren't happy you're going to all these witnesses behind our backs. You're tampering with an active case." The anger in James's voice was evident. "What else?"

I sighed and finished my tea. We stared at each other. The lines between his eyes deepened. I sighed again.

"Tom drugged women, slept with them, and took pictures for his Body Count book."

"A Body Count book?" James said, sitting upright in the chair as if he wanted to leave. "Where's it now?"

I explained where he could find it and gave him a short version of what Lucky had told me about Tom and those special drugs, but didn't divulge too much about Miguel, only that their supplier made it themselves. To save my skin, I needed Donnie and James to investigate Miguel's drug making on their own. Miguel might've indicated he didn't kill, but one never truly knew, and I'd be the first person he'd think of. I also didn't share what Lucky had told me about that man who bought the drugs from him; I wanted to first find out who he was. I knew it was wrong, but I needed to know if he had a direct connection to Tom or Pam, and why he needed those special pills.

"Your brother and I aren't happy you're doing this." His smile didn't reach his eyes.

"I'm sorry," I said; the guilt rearing its ugly head. "Are you disappointed?"

"I get why, but it feels as though there's something wrong with our relationship, you know, that you felt you couldn't come to me when Pam did. Were you in the apartment the morning of?"

I pursed my lips.

"Dana." He rubbed his face. "Did you touch anything?"

"No, yes," I said, cringing. "I wiped down the areas I touched."

"That's tampering with a crime scene. It could've had the actual killer's prints."

"I know." I sounded dejected. "When I arrived at the apartment, I didn't know what was going on until I saw all the blood and by then I'd already touched the door. Pam panicked. I panicked. I did what I thought was right."

"We're still waiting for the results. I hope they find nothing of yours." We were quiet for a moment. "Where's Pam?" he asked again.

"I don't know. Truly. She's meant to phone me soon."

"When she does, you must tell us where she is. We need to get her side of the story."

Chapter Twenty-Five

DONNIE

"THANKS FOR THE COFFEE," I said, enjoying a sip.

"What?" James stared at me as if he were about to say something but kept stopping himself.

"Your sister."

"Is the P.I. asking questions."

"Yeah, I spoke to her about it last night," James said, not sounding happy, and I wondered if their relationship took a knock because of it. I wouldn't ask though; it was none of my business, but I'd find out soon if she'd done any damage to their marriage.

"Man, I know her too well," I said. "I don't like that she's interfering where she's not wanted. I get Pam is her friend and she wants to help her, but this is the wrong way to go about doing it."

"There's something else." James added with a serious tone he hardly used.

"Spit it out."

"Tom has a Body Count book where he puts pictures of the women he'd drugged and slept with."

"Of course he does." I said, relieved we had more evidence but also sickened by what this guy had been up to. A man who needed to drug women and took pictures of them was up there with pedophiles. At least now we had something that could assist us in finding the killer. "Where is it?"

"His apartment."

"Let's grab it on our way to Bev," I said, grabbing my keys.

We found the book where Dana had said it would be, and to say how disgusted I was, was an understatement. The book was horrific. It was obvious Tom had drugged the women in these photos, and they were all in various stages of undress. In some photos there was blood; nothing in others.

"I hope he didn't film any of this," James said, stopping at the last page.

"I think the team needs to return and see if there's any other hidden compartments or cameras. One good thing is we now have a motive."

"Yeah, and hey, at least he'd fallen in love with Pam." James tapped on the picture of Pam, which was dated Friday.

"It doesn't matter. If he were still alive and Pam found out, she'd drop his ass, and if she didn't, Dana would make her." I chuckled at the thought. My sister, I loved her most days yet sometimes I wanted to slap her when she got under my skin like now, but she also protected those she cared about, and it was obvious she cared about Pam.

James chuckled. "Yeah, I have no doubt she'd do that."

"Go through all the pages just in case," I said.

James paged through, and then right at the back was a

picture of Tom and Pam asleep. "No blood," he said. "Someone took this picture before stabbing Tom."

"At least we kind of have proof Pam was asleep since she's in the picture, and they both look drugged." I narrowed my eyes at the photograph, at the clock on the bedside table, which read 2 a.m. "Did you see a picture of Bev?"

"Oh yeah, it's here," James paged back and stopped where a girl with curly brown hair lay on her stomach, her face turned away from the camera. She was naked, and there was a bloody handprint on her back. "He must've hurt her badly to leave so much blood."

Under the picture Tom had written; *"I smashed Bev's tight holes."*

It disgusted me to see these pictures and even more so to read what Tom had written. Those poor women had gone through so much. It was a blessing they couldn't remember what he'd done to them.

———

WE ARRIVED at Bev's house after lunch. We traversed up the path towards the front door. There were children's toys strewn all over the neat lawn, and a sprayer was on in the far corner. I knocked on the door.

"Coming," a woman yelled. The door opened, and a woman with rosy, chubby cheeks smiled; the dimples in her cheeks dented, making her look younger than she was.

"Beverly Newman?" James said.

"Yes," she said, her eyes flitting from James to me.

We introduced ourselves. She flinched when we showed her our badges.

"Would you like something to drink?" she asked, leaving the door open for us.

We sat in the living room drinking our coffee. Beverly sat in a chair large enough to hold her weight. She was at least four times the size of the girl we'd seen in the Body Count book. I felt sorry for her; no woman should go through something so traumatic.

"Thanks for the coffee," I said, smiling. "The reason we're here is to ask you a few questions about Tom Westbrook—"

The cup and saucer in Beverly's hand clanked against each other, her hand trembling. She swallowed hard and set the cup and saucer on the table beside her, spilling drops of tea. "Tom…" she coughed. "Tom. Um, why do you want to talk about Tom? I hadn't heard that name in years."

"Someone murdered Tom—"

She gasped, covering her mouth with both shaky hands. "Murdered." She blinked slowly as she processed the information and exhaled. She visibly relaxed and sighed.

"We understand he hurt women," I continued. "And we've been told that he might've hurt you."

She nodded as tears welled in her eyes. She blinked, and the tears fell down her cheeks, which she promptly dusted off. "I won't lie, I'm glad he's dead. He was not a nice person. I'm sure you've heard the things he's done?"

"We've heard some stories. We spoke with Tom's ex-colleague—"

"Elizabeth?"

I nodded.

"Did he hurt her, too? I can't believe it. When I last saw her, she said nothing. No wonder it seemed like she wanted to say something but then kept quiet."

"We'd like to hear your version of the story," James added.

She nodded and dusted more tears off her cheeks. I suspected those were tears of relief, and her healing could properly begin now.

"Okay, I met Tom one Friday evening. I'd been going to the warehouse with my girlfriends for a few months, spoke to Elizabeth often, and had only ever seen Tom walking around greeting everyone. I later found out he was dealing drugs; that's why it looked like he was a social butterfly. Anyway, my friend wanted to party one evening, and we flagged Tom down and asked him to get some stuff for us. For some reason, he took a liking to me."

Beverly picked up her tea cup and took a few sips. We waited patiently. When she was done, she continued speaking, "Tom was very charming, had this amazing energy that was above and beyond; made me feel like I was the only woman in his world. He made me feel so good; gave me lots of compliments, showered me with affection. His words were so smooth, but I was too blind to see it when I was in his orbit. He offered me an ecstasy tablet that looked like the others. I'd tried it before, so I knew what to expect, but *that* pill," she shook her head. "That pill made me lose my mind so easily and quickly. One moment I was on the dance floor with my friends and Tom was beside me; the next thing it was Saturday morning, and I was naked in his bed covered in blood."

"Was he home when you woke up?" I asked.

"Yes, brought me coffee in bed. He was full of smiles and even kissed my temple. He continued with his act the entire time, making me feel comfortable, or rather keeping me docile so that I didn't freak out and accuse him of things I couldn't remember, except I felt it in my body. I knew something bad had happened; something was wrong." She choked back a sob.

"Could you remember anything?" James asked.

"Months later, I kept getting flashbacks of memories I couldn't place until I realized I remembered that night. He had used a condom and had assaulted me both vaginally and anally. He was rough, like he had become a wild animal, but he did it in such a way that I couldn't really feel it the next day. I wasn't that sore, even though there was blood and I felt different. I don't know how to explain it, but I knew something had happened, but it wasn't serious enough because there were no tears." She blushed as she recounted what had happened.

It saddened me to listen to what Bev had gone through. A man hurting a woman this badly should suffer for his actions. However, it relieved me Tom was gone and would hurt no one again.

"We understand," I said, making a note. "Do you remember anything else? Did you hear of it happening to someone else we could speak to, or can you think of someone who may have wanted him dead?"

"I wanted him dead, but it wasn't me." She suppressed a smile. "But to answer your question, I know of no one else who could hurt him."

Chapter Twenty-Six

DANA

I WAS YET to hear from Pam. While I waited, I needed to speak with her husband; perhaps he knew something I didn't. I hoped Pam wouldn't reach out to him because everything could come crashing down on her if she did.

I watched the children leave for school, then I traversed up the path and knocked on the front door.

Ethan opened the door and frowned when he saw me. "Can I help you?"

I couldn't be sure, and I didn't want to check my phone, but Ethan looked like that man Lucky had pointed out. Not wanting to arouse suspicion, I swallowed my thoughts and opened my mouth to talk. "Hi, I'm Dana Mulder, and I'm looking for your wife."

"Me included. Why are you looking for her?" He asked suspiciously.

"I'm busy investigating the death of someone and need to question her."

"I don't know what happened," he said, his words clipped, and tone raised. "And I don't know where Pam is. I didn't even know she was having an affair. There, does that sum it up for you?" He was about to close the door when I stuck my foot out.

"Before you go," I said, wincing from the pain. He opened the door wider and sighed audibly. "Don't you think that perhaps someone might have drugged her?"

"Drugged?" he said. "What makes you think that?"

"She remembers nothing of the evening."

"So you *have* spoken to her." He narrowed his eyes.

"She told me what happened, and I've been trying to help her."

His shoulders tensed. "What did she say?" He folded his arms across his chest.

"She saw you at the warehouse and had bought drugs." I was lying; Pam told me nothing about seeing him, but Lucky did, and I needed to see Ethan's reaction; he flinched and then quickly schooled his features. "And that you were there with a blonde woman."

"She's lying," he said, his eyes looking everywhere except at me. "Pam is unstable, crazy, said I hurt her. Stole my money. She needs help. When you speak to her again, tell her to go to a hospital, and I'll make sure she's taken care of." He slammed the door in my face so quickly I didn't have time to react; I also didn't want him breaking my foot.

I left his home and went to the gym. I couldn't remember that woman's name and hoped I'd bump into her here. Swiping my card and entering, I headed for the yoga studio. The morning class had just ended; I waited, watching the women leave one by one, and when I recognized the blonde from the other day, I grabbed her upper arm.

"Excuse me," I said, pulling her towards me and out of the way. "We need to talk."

"What? Why?" she asked, glancing around as if she were about to call for help.

"What's your name?" I asked, smiling sweetly, trying to put her at ease. "I saw you the other day and wanted to say hi, but I'd forgotten who you were, but I know you're Pam's friend."

"Yes, that's right. I'm Julia." She relaxed. "I've seen you two hang out together."

"Julia, yes. Now I remember." I eased my grip on her arm and nodded. "Does your husband know you're having an affair with Pam's husband?"

Her body stiffened. "I don't know what you're talking about." She turned and headed for the exit.

"What does this look like to you?" I asked, shoving my phone in her face. "That is you, isn't it?"

Julia stopped dead and reached for my phone.

"No," I said, pulling it away and sticking it in my bag. "Talk to me."

We sat at the health bar restaurant inside the gym, each drinking mocha tea; her treat.

"I met Ethan when Pam and I were out for lunch. He needed to give her money to pay the bills. The next day he sought me out and asked me if I wanted to join him for coffee. I said no initially, but he was insistent."

"Why? You have a husband who gives you everything. Pam and Ethan are also happily married." I knew they weren't, but I needed to understand how much Julia knew about what went on between them.

"He'd fallen out of love with Pam. Said their relationship was over, doomed, and he wanted to divorce her. He had started the proceedings with a lawyer already. And I guess I fell in love with him and had spoken with a lawyer too. My husband is old and wouldn't be around much longer. The difference between us is my husband knows about my lovers, so I didn't really need to divorce him. Ethan didn't like that because he wanted us to marry. Anyway, we're busy working that part out."

"Have you seen the divorce papers he wants to give Pam?"

She shook her head. "No, not yet. He said there was something about the assets he still wanted to sort out. I don't know the details; I didn't want to talk about it."

"Do you think Ethan can hurt someone?"

"No," she said, frowning. "I heard about what happened to Tom, and no, I don't think he could've done that. It sounded like quite a violent death."

It amazed me how fast news travelled. "Do you know anyone who might have wanted Tom dead?"

"No, Tom was such a great guy. He had good energy, you know."

That seemed to be the main thing about him; his energy. I understood why everyone thought that; he was charismatic. He wore the broadest smile, was super friendly, and he made you feel special. We'd only interacted a couple of times, but I struggled to enjoy his company; I always felt exhausted and dirty afterwards without understanding why. At first, I couldn't place it, only that I didn't enjoy spending time around him. Perhaps it was the darkness I saw in his eyes, or those bushy eyebrows, that smile that didn't seem genuine, or his perfect words that didn't match his actions; whatever it was my nervous system knew something was off about him.

When Pam told me how much she liked him, it shocked me. I never would've imagined this. Then I thought about it and realized it could be a good thing for both. She'd have someone to take her mind off Ethan, and perhaps Tom would be a better man. I wanted my sixth sense to be wrong about him since I was the only one who felt that way. If only I'd known about his background, I could've helped Pam avoid all this. In hindsight, I should've done a background check on him, but I didn't know; I couldn't run around doing checks on everybody.

I learned a lesson and that I should always trust my intuition. *Always*.

Chapter Twenty-Seven

DONNIE

"SORRY FOR THE DELAY," Dr. Warryn said, pushing his glasses up his nose to read from the report. Today he wore suspender belts to keep his navy pants up, a neatly pressed white shirt, a light blue bowtie, and his white lab coat to finish the look. "I thought I'd be done in a day, but then I got sidetracked by another death and another," he shrugged. "It never ends. There's always someone dying and every autopsy is urgent." He shook his head.

"No worries, Doc," I said. "What do you have for us?"

"Okay," he continued reading from the report. "Your victim, Tom Westbrook, aged thirty-five, was in good health apart from liver and kidney damage. Do you know if he was an alcoholic or drug user?" He asked, glancing between James and me.

"Both," we said at the same time.

"Makes sense," Dr. Warryn continued reading. "His kidneys and liver were so badly damaged I doubt he would've made it to fifty. There were two deep lacerations on his neck, severing his carotid artery, causing him to bleed to death quickly."

"Two?" James said, looking confused; as was I.

"Yes, I'll show you shortly. I found a cut on his C4 vertebra. The knife used was very sharp, but it wasn't the knife found at the scene."

"That's surprising," I said, making a note. "Do you have any idea what kind?"

"No, only that it was extremely sharp, small enough to pierce the skin and cut the spine. A scalpel, maybe."

I made a note; perhaps it was someone medically trained to use a scalpel.

"Were there any other traces?"

"The handprint on his back was too smudged to get any prints," Dr. Warryn said. "He'd had sexual relations with an unknown woman. We found semen on the bedsheets and vaginal lubrication on his penis. He also had scratch marks down his back, which I attribute to the sexual activity before his death. Toxicology came back, and we found traces of Rohypnol, GHB, and an unknown extract we're trying to decipher. I suspect it's some natural ingredient, but I'll let you know once I know."

James and I made notes of everything while Dr. Warryn removed the sheet so we could see Tom's body. Dr. Warryn had sewn the Y-incision closed but left the deep gash in Tom's neck open for us to see. It wasn't just a cut; it was as if the person wanted to gouge out his spine. I glanced down the rest of Tom's body, realizing why he had big-dick energy; he was certainly blessed in that department.

I leaned closer to get a better look at his neck. "Jeez, I see what you mean. It's like they tried to operate on him. I mean, I can see his spine from here. It didn't look this bad when he was in bed."

"No, they cut him once across his throat, then vertically to open the wound further, then they closed it again, making it look like a small incision until I got him here and noticed how large it was."

He motioned for us to help move Tom's body onto its side, pointing out the large purple bruise on his back. "I think someone kneeled on his back, keeping him down while they sliced his neck."

Seeing the bruises on Tom's back made sense; it was also proof that someone bigger kept Tom in place. Pam was as short as Dana, and I doubted she did it. James glanced at me, and we shared a knowing look; he didn't think Pam did it either.

A cool wind caressed my cheek, making me shiver. We lowered Tom's body onto his back once more, and Doc covered him.

"I've sent you a copy of my findings. Good luck." And with his parting words, he exited out the back and to his office.

———

WE HADN'T SPOKEN with Lucky yet and headed for his apartment after meeting with Dr. Warryn. Clouds gathered overhead, bringing a cold wind. I huddled in my jacket as we entered the building with the painted squirrel on one side.

Two knocks on Lucky's door and he answered. "Yeah?" he asked, pinching one eye closed and glaring at us with the other one. "What do you want?"

We raised our badges for him to see. "We'd like to speak with you about Tom Westbrook."

"Not you as well. Can't you just speak to that other girl?" He mumbled as he opened the door.

We entered the messy apartment, watching him hide the weed, white powder, and pipes, but that's not why we were here. We'd let our narcotics division know about this, but they'd most likely want the guy at the top and not Lucky.

This was as neat as the apartment was ever going to get, so we sat across from him. The couch squeaked on my end; I prayed the spring didn't release and stab me in the ass.

"Who's this girl asking questions?" I already knew it was my pain-in-the-ass-sister, but I needed to hear it from him.

"Dana somebody," Lucky said with a sigh. "I can't remember everything I told her," he rubbed his face, "I tried this new stuff, and, you know, it kinda blew my mind wide open. Anyway, I remember telling her about Tom. I think I have her card around here somewhere." He glanced around, pushing books and papers off the coffee table, and a glass clanked against an old bottle and it almost fell to the floor.

"Don't worry about the card," I said, motioning him to stop.

"Why don't you tell us?" James said, pushing a wet cloth off his side of the couch and onto the floor. I cringed. James paled. The sooner we got this over with, the better. "Tell us about Tom. We're not here to arrest you for using and dealing drugs. We want to know what happened to Tom."

With another big sigh, Lucky told us he and Tom went to school together, as we'd read in the various arrest reports. When they were still in school, they only sold weed, and after they left school, they sold cocaine and heroin. When they worked at the warehouse, they sold ecstasy. Tom was always a bit of a player and could be seen with a new girl every week. Then Lucky went into depth about Tom drugging the women and creating a Body Count book.

"We've seen the book," James said.

"Then you know what a shit Tom was. Whoever killed him did every lady a service. He was bad news, man. He might've said he changed for that Pam chick, but I know him; he never would've changed. There's always some young girl out there he wants to taste, you know. That guy could never keep it in his pants; would fuck his problems away with that big dick of his. He was always chasing instant gratification, the thrill, the excitement, until he gets it and then he loses interest."

"Do you know what happened to him when he was a kid?" I asked.

"His uncle molested him when he was like five; soon thereafter his dad left, then his mom died, and they put him with the same uncle because nobody else claimed him. It was torture for Tom. I think Tom even killed his uncle because one day the guy just died. Dead. Just like that, and nobody knows how." Lucky snapped his fingers.

"Do you know anyone who wanted to kill Tom?"

"Shit man, lots of folks. Pick a number. All the women he used. Anyone, none of them. Your guess is as good as mine." He sniffed hard and swallowed.

It was hopeless trying to get detailed information out of Lucky, so we ended the interview.

"What do you think?" James asked, starting the ignition, and the car roared to life.

"Have we been able to track down Pam?"

"No, her cellphone has been off since Saturday. Her husband hasn't seen her, and he's stressed because their children aren't coping."

"Did you phone him?"

"Yep, when I tried her number again this morning, I called him."

"We need to speak with Dana," I said. "And afterwards I'm going to kill her for going behind our backs in an active murder investigation."

Chapter Twenty-Eight

PAM

TOM HOVERED ABOVE ME. His smile splitting his face in two. He leaned forward and kissed me. "You're everything I've always wanted," he said between thrusts.

"Really?" I said, not quite believing him. I enjoyed the sensation of his body as he made love to me.

"Yes, I've been waiting for someone like you to come into my life for a long time."

"But we hardly know each other."

Tom always said the right words, and I couldn't help but feel like he said these to every woman in his bed.

"There are things I've done in my life I'm not proud of and no longer want to do. I can't erase my past, but going forward I can make things right. Since I've known you, I want to be a better man; I want to man up for you," he said breathlessly. He stilled, leaned forward and kissed me passionately.

His touch and kisses were heavenly. It felt wonderful being in his embrace as we made love. This wasn't just sex, this was true love; I couldn't explain why I thought that, I just knew it.

I awoke gasping for air and glanced around; I was at Mom's house and not in Tom's bed. It was a dream, just a dream, yet it felt so real. It felt like a memory of our one and only night together. I sat up, my skin damp, and my heart raced. There was something else in that dream, a darkness in the corner watching us. Perhaps it was my brain trying to make sense of everything, imagining the killer was there in the room with us, waiting for us to finish and fall asleep before killing Tom.

I remembered what he'd said to me about wanting to change his life, and I remembered how I'd felt in that moment. I didn't know what to think at first and decided to give him the benefit of the doubt. That I'd believe his words and would trust him when his actions matched. It was one thing professing his love for me; it was a whole different ball game doing those things. I'd learned a lot from my years of marriage to Ethan.

The vision of Tom kept flashing before my eyes and how I'd felt in that moment. It happened; it was real and not a dream. He'd said those things to me, and I'd felt that way.

My stomach pained, reminding me of the butterflies I had when Tom texted me. I realized now that it wasn't butterflies, it wasn't excitement, but my body telling me that seeing Tom could be dangerous. It was my nervous system letting me know that meeting Tom would be a bad idea; if only I'd known the difference between butterflies and warning, all of this could've been avoided.

I also needed to eat something and get my mind off these visions and feelings. I ate the last of my toast and finished my coffee. The air conditioner rattled overhead, and cars drove past outside my mom's house. A couple of women fast-walked around the neighborhood. I watched this unfold, my mind replaying the dream, while my leg continued bouncing up and down and my fingers fidgeted with my sleeves. I'd bitten my nails short, and I stank; I hadn't had a shower since Saturday afternoon, and it was Tuesday already.

Rubbing my eyes, I decided I needed to take charge of my life, take back control, and go back to Chicago to see what's going on. I couldn't just hang around here and wait for feedback, even though Dana had instructed me to do so.

I sighed.

I had to listen to her, but my children; I missed them. I choked on a sob thinking about my three kids, and now I was desperate to get home for their hugs.

After a quick shower, I packed a backpack and the rest of the money and called a cab. The twenty-minute ride to Chicago felt like hours. Dana had given me her work address, and I waited outside for her to arrive. It was ten o'clock when a BMW I recognized parked outside the office and she climbed out.

"Pam!" she yelled, then quickly glanced around. "What are you doing here?" she whispered. "I told you to wait."

"I know, and I'm sorry," I said, blinking back tears. I hugged her and gave in to the emotions, wetting her shoulder. "Sorry, it's just that I want to see my kids. I miss my family. I want to speak to Ethan—"

"Stop," she said firmly. "You are putting your life in danger by coming here. I told you I was working on things, and I am. My brother and James are working on your case, and they don't think you're involved. So, relax. And seeing your kids will only upset you further. Now come inside before someone sees you."

A cold, sinking feeling set in my bones as I entered her office. *Had anyone seen me?* I glanced around nervously but saw no one.

Dana had a small waiting area with a sofa, a tiny kitchenette, her office, and a bathroom. She made us coffee, and we sat in her office.

"You shouldn't have come here," she said delicately. "I've managed to get information and have passed it on to James and Donnie, and they're handling things. We'll find the person responsible. I promise you." She fell silent while we drank our coffee. It looked like she wanted to say something else.

"What is it?" I asked, trying desperately to stop my hands from shaking. "There's something you're not telling me."

She leaned back in her chair, staring hard at me. "What I'm about to tell you will come out anyway, but I'm not sure now is the right time."

"Please tell me. I need to know. I can handle it." After I said those words, I wondered whether I could handle it; then again, I'd woken up beside a dead man and covered in his blood. Then I cleaned parts of the crime scene and hid away. I could handle anything now.

"Tom wasn't a great guy, Pam. He was awful."

My spine stiffened. "What do you mean?" My frown deepened, and the muscles in my neck spasmed. "I don't understand what you're telling me."

"He used to drug women then had sex with them."

Ice filled my veins, and my limbs went numb. The coffee mug slipped out of my hands and crashed to the floor, spilling the contents. "Sorry. Um, it's not broken."

"It's okay. Did you get hurt?"

"No," I said, bending to pick up the mug. I moved hair

out of my face, quickly dusting the tear away. "What are you saying? That he drugged me that night on purpose?"

"No, maybe," she said. "I think this time he didn't. That maybe someone else drugged you two."

"I'm not following." A pain in my chest blossomed.

"Tom really liked you and wanted to change his ways for you."

When she said that, I thought back to the dream I had where Tom had said he'd done some things. Perhaps that's what he'd meant; that he was remorseful for all the bad things he'd done.

"He wanted to build a life with you. I think someone gave Tom pills laced with something else. There's no way Tom would do that to himself or to you."

I opened my mouth unsure of what to say. "I should've gone to the hospital for tests, but I was too afraid."

"I know," Dana said, comforting me. "It was too risky at the time. We had to be sure you were safe first, and I needed to figure things out."

"Now what?"

"Wait," she raised her hand, "there's more."

My stomach dropped to my toes, and the back of my throat ached. The pain in my chest grew.

"Tom had a Body Count book where he put pictures of all the women he did this to."

Disappointed wasn't the right word for how I was feeling; cheated, lied to, betrayed, disgusted. I didn't trust my voice to answer and stared at her.

"There's more."

"No," I said, standing and pacing. "What the… it's like I didn't know him at all."

"This time it's your husband."

I stopped pacing and stared at her. "What? Ethan?

What about Ethan?" I sat down again, bracing myself for more bad news.

"I'm sorry to have to tell you after all the other terrible news, but I was right. Ethan was cheating on you with Julia—"

"I knew it!" I yelled, fisting my hands. "That mother-fu…" I hated swearing and desperately wanted to scream into the void until I lost my voice. I couldn't believe this was happening, yet I could. "It's as if I knew nothing about those closest to me. I was so blinded by my life and thoughts that I didn't see what was right in front of me. How long had the affair been going on?"

"Julia told me it started six months ago."

Tears welled in my eyes. The pain in my chest spread to my back, and I wanted to crawl into the corner and cry or maybe even die. Perhaps I should give up and end it all, but my children. I wanted my kids. I needed to see my children. "My life just turned to shit, Dana. What the… I don't know what to do now." I stood and paced.

"Nothing. Do nothing, Pam. Go back to where you came from, and I'll handle everything. I'll call you when things settle down and we have the killer."

"Do you know who the killer might be?"

She shook her head.

"Any suspects?"

"One or two, we're still investigating." She stood and approached me, putting her arms around my shoulders and hugging me hard. She shouldn't have done that because the moment I felt her tenderness, I broke down. I wrapped my arms around her waist and cried.

"Thank you for being in my corner," I said between sobs. "You're like the only person on my side. The only person dedicated to helping me get out of this shitstorm. I can't believe what you told me. A Body Count book? Really? Like why? So he could enjoy the trauma he caused, reliving it as he paged through the book. I'm so dumb for falling for him."

"He was good at getting women to trust him. Don't beat yourself up; it happened to so many. They all fell for his charm. He's just one of those guys who has a magnetic pull, and you lose yourself when you're close to him. You can't think clearly, and you believe everything he tells you. It was a hard lesson, but you're alive and can move on."

"And Ethan... I mean, no wonder he's been so distant. It explains everything." It also explained why he hurt me so badly that night after he ripped my underwear off. He'd never been that rough with me before. I wondered if he was rough like that with Julia; no, I didn't want to know.

"I'm so sorry," she added. "All this is a hard pill to swallow, especially now. Go back and let me finish this for you. It will all be okay."

I wiped the tears off my face with the back of my sleeve. "I want to divorce the asshole and take everything I can get. It's going to cost him everything. And the contract we signed before we got married says if he cheats, I get the house, the car, everything he bought me, and half of his money and future income."

She raised both eyebrows. "Future income?"

"Yeah, I gave up so much for him while he studied, so I made him put in that clause that says if he cheats on me or wants to divorce me, he has to give me half his paycheck every month until one of us dies."

She stared knowingly at me, but I didn't understand. "What?"

"Ethan was at the club on Friday."

Chapter Twenty-Nine

DANA

ON ONE HAND, I appreciated Pam coming through to see me, but I also didn't like it. However, she provided me with vital information about their prenup, and Ethan was at the warehouse on Friday, and he got those specific drugs from Lucky. The coincidence was too much to ignore. But what I couldn't understand was how Ethan swapped those drugs with the ones Lucky had given Tom.

Before speaking to Ethan again, I needed more information and did an in-depth search on him. He was high up the corporate ladder at a marketing company; top management with some wonderful perks and a bonus check that would make anyone's eyes pop out of their heads if the information online was to be believed. It was a lot of money. He also held shares in various companies that totaled over a million dollars according to another financial website I had access to. Pam would take half of everything. It was motive to get rid of her, except he didn't kill her; he killed Tom, which made little sense. He was cheating on her and would divorce her, losing half of everything. It was the perfect opportunity to get rid of her and Tom.

This told me Tom was always the target. Pam was just collateral damage. Unless Ethan wanted Pam to be accused of the murder and to go to prison, when he divorced her she got nothing. That made sense. It reminded me of a neatly tied ribbon around a present. He pinned the perfect murder on Pam and could wipe his hands clean.

Except... he didn't anticipate I'd help her. That I would figure it out and take this to my brother and husband. I smiled at the thought of seeing Ethan's shocked face when I revealed this to him.

I needed to first question him and hear his side of the story. I should just give this information to my husband, but something was gnawing at me, and I wanted to hear directly from Ethan.

I knocked on his front door when I knew he was home alone. As much as I didn't want to be alone with him, I didn't want his kids hearing our conversation.

He yanked the door open and glowered down at me. "What now? Haven't you done enough?"

"I spoke with Pam," I said, pausing.

His features softened for a moment. "Where is she?"

"Don't know," I said, meaning it. I didn't know where she was, although I had my suspicions.

"What do you want from me?"

"I know about the affair with Julia."

He didn't flinch, didn't look away, nothing. He stared down at me as if I were a bug on his shoe.

"Why poison them?" I continued. "Why kill only Tom? You should've killed Pam as well, then she wouldn't take half of your assets during the divorce."

His frown deepened. "What are you going on about? I

didn't kill Tom, and I certainly wouldn't hurt my wife. I was cheating on her; I think that's bad enough. There's no need to hurt her or her lover, which I knew nothing about until a couple of days ago."

He was a good liar.

"You were at the club on Friday." I'd already accused him of this, and he slammed the door in my face, but now I had a witness. "Julia confirmed this."

He sighed. "You've spoken to her?"

"Yes. You two bought drugs and partied like teenagers. The dealer pointed you out, said you almost attacked him trying to get the drugs."

"I didn't attack him, and he's lying." He leaned against the doorjamb. "I bought from him, and yes, we took. We only had one each even though I got six. I hadn't taken recreational drugs since my college years, and I felt ill; you can ask Julia. We went home early, and I was throwing up for the rest of the evening, in and out of consciousness."

I didn't know whether to believe him and would ask Julia, but I'd need proof because they could've done this together and Julia could lie to protect Ethan.

"If you'll excuse me, I must get to a work meeting." He closed the door, stomping across the floor until I could no longer hear him.

Chapter Thirty

DONNIE

"I'M ANGRY WITH YOU," I said, pointing my finger at Dana.

She folded her arms across her chest and leaned back in the chair. "I had to."

"You are messing with an active investigation."

She raised her hands in mock surrender. "Sorry, I didn't mean to, but I came forward when I found things you guys needed to know."

"Only because James pushed you for answers."

She sighed. "Sorry." Her eyes flitted from James to me.

"You need to stop doing this."

"I haven't done this in years, Donnie."

It was my turn to sigh. "I know, but still. You should've come to us first with Pam, so we could sort it out. She didn't have to run away."

She pursed her lips, glancing at her shaking leg. "Everybody runs, Donnie. Especially the innocent ones."

"Where is she?"

"I honestly don't know. Told her not to tell me."

"Do you at least have a number you can reach her on?"

She averted her eyes.

"Dana."

"Okay, fine, I have a number for her, but I'll only give it to you once you have a suspect." The lines between her eyes deepened. "Do you have a suspect?"

"Either Elizabeth Marconi or Lucky."

She shook her head. "Look at her husband. He's having an affair with Julia. Pam told me she gets half of everything in the divorce and future money."

"Did you know this?" I asked James.

"No," James said.

"You need to question Ethan and Julia and find out exactly what they did Friday night," she said.

Chapter Thirty-One

PAM

I COULDN'T BELIEVE Ethan was at the club on Friday. I knew I'd seen Julia; or someone similar but thought I was hallucinating. Now I understood why. It's because she was there with my husband. *Had he seen us?* He must've. Then he followed us to Tom's place, where he killed Tom after we fell asleep. Ethan wanted me to go to jail for a crime he committed just so that he wouldn't have to pay out during the divorce. He was so selfish. He was the one having the affair yet made me feel like I was losing my mind when I questioned him about us.

Where had things gone so wrong between us? I'd loved Ethan, and I knew he'd loved me too. But when did we lose that love for each other? I knew it happened slowly and over years; but when exactly? It was something I had to accept; it was a sad moment and a part of my life I needed to mourn.

I bolted upright when I saw Ethan exit his place of work with Julia. They held hands and smiled and looked in love, like the world was at their feet. Yet here I was in turmoil with my life about to be destroyed for something I didn't commit. Anger flooded my veins as I watched them. They were happy, madly in love and about to live the life that was mine; that used to be me with Ethan.

"Please follow that car," I said to the cab driver.

"Yes, Ma'am." The driver merged into traffic and followed Ethan's sleek black Mercedes. They went to *my* home, holding hands as they traversed up the path to *my* front door. "Where to next?" The driver asked.

"Thanks," I said, giving him cash. "You can drop me off here."

"You sure?" he said. "Is that man your husband?"

I stared daggers at him; it wasn't his business. Then I sighed sadly, feeling instantly guilty for taking my mood out on the cab driver, and I hadn't even said anything to him.

"You want my card, then you phone me to take you somewhere else?"

"Yeah, please," I said, reaching for his card and pocketing it. "Thanks."

I stood on my lawn and stared at the house I shared with Ethan. I *used* to share. The thing that hurt the most, apart from the betrayal, was my children. They knew nothing about what had happened or how Ethan had cheated on me for six months. To be fair, I slept with someone too, but only once, and then someone had killed him in the same bed we shared for one night. I might need therapy for the rest of my life after everything that had happened.

I entered my house quietly, listening for where they were. Bedroom. I should've known. The noises stopped. I went into the kitchen and then traversed the stairs quietly. Nearing my bedroom, I carefully peered inside, watching them snuggle each other and fall asleep. At least they had a satisfactory late-afternoon date. The kids weren't home from school. Nobody would see me. I wanted to hurt them both, wanted them to bleed like Tom had bled. Tom was a terrible man for hurting so many women, but what Ethan did was worse, and I wanted him out of my life, out of my kids' lives. I wanted him gone.

Their breathing became heavier as they slept. I entered the room, observing them, ensuring they didn't wake.

I stood at the foot of the king-size bed I shared with Ethan. It had only been ten years since we bought the bed, but I remembered that day like it was yesterday; it was a beautiful summer morning when we were still happily in love and wanted to spend the rest of our lives together; or so I'd thought.

A cool breeze moved the white curtains, making me shiver. I watched him sleep. His chest rising and falling as he dreamed peacefully. It was a stark contrast to my emotions; anger, hate, fury, contempt. The list went on.

Ghostly children's laughter echoed around the room as I recalled our three kids sneaking into our bedroom and climbing under the comforter to snuggle with us. Those were the best times of my life; when things were good and my life *was* perfect.

But nothing stayed perfect, no matter how hard I tried.

I could never understand how anyone could hurt the person they loved. How was it possible to go from loving someone so deeply to hating them with every fiber of your being? I understood that now, but it came at a cost to me. A cost that almost ended my life.

My breath hitched as I blinked, a tear slipping down my cheek. My veins heated as I squeezed the hilt of the sharp knife; my hand pained. My chest ached as the love that used to live there had dissolved by betrayal, leaving behind a hole. We used to be so happy together and shared many wonderful memories. I loved him so much and would've done anything for him. Now… now there was nothing but an emptiness that could never be replaced or filled no matter what he said or did.

Now… there was only one way… *till death do us part.*

I stared down at him as I considered my options.

Should I stab him in his chest or neck first?

Should I stab her? The woman sleeping with my husband.

I wanted them both to hurt, to bleed, to die. But those weren't my sane thoughts. I could never hurt someone like that; I wasn't a monster. I couldn't hurt anyone no matter how angry I was, even though I wanted them to feel what I went through. I was better than that. My mother said I was a good girl; I was a good person who always put others first. This wasn't who I wanted to be; I didn't want to hurt anyone.

I swallowed hard watching my husband sleep soundlessly with his lover and stepped away, squeezing the hilt of the knife in my hand until my knuckles hurt.

I called the number on the card, and the cab driver said he'd be there in twenty minutes. I stood at the farthest corner away from the house and waited for him.

As I climbed into the cab, Ethan stood in the bedroom window and stared at me. Normally I wouldn't think anything of it, but it was the way he stared at me. There was so much hate behind his eyes it left a stain on my skin.

I slammed the cab door closed. "Get out of here," I said harshly, then gave the driver the address to my mother's home. As we went past the house, Ethan continued to stare, then he disappeared, but it still felt as though he was watching.

Chapter Thirty-Two

PAM

BEFORE HEADING HOME, we stopped at the store for milk and some groceries. Once back at Mom's place, I thanked the cab driver and gave him a handsome tip for putting me at ease after seeing Ethan stare at me like that. Ethan had never made me feel that uncomfortable before, other than the night he tore my underwear and we had rough sex. Ethan was always gentle with me, kind, compassionate. Now I hardly knew him; he was a different person; someone I didn't want to know.

At least I was home; it was my mom's home but still, a home away from home, and I was safe here. I threw my handbag on the couch, entered the kitchen to pack away the groceries and poured myself the largest glass of red wine. I had to first sip carefully not to spill. As I sat on the sofa with my feet up and the glass in my hand, I kept replaying the moment I stood in my bedroom holding a knife and wanting to cut my husband and his mistress to him staring at me with murderous intent. It was unsettling, so I needed to forget it and move on. I needed to get out of this mess first.

"Are you safe?" Dana messaged.

"Yes, back at Mom's place. Are you close to catching the killer?"

"Almost."

"Who?"

She didn't respond, and I didn't double-text. I'd leave it for now. For an hour or two, I wanted to forget about Ethan, forget about Tom's lifeless body next to mine, and just drink my wine.

Unfortunately, no matter what I tried, my mind kept going back to that night. Memories of that evening surfaced, and they were of Tom's naked body on mine. His full lips kissing mine. His hands were all over my body like he couldn't get enough of me. I wanted that night to carry on forever, and I wanted us to last forever too. But what messed with me the most was the things he'd done to all those women; that a man like him needed to drug someone to have sex with them. His charm fooled me; just like every other girl he interacted with. There was nothing wrong with them, nothing wrong with me; it was all on Tom. There was a lot going on in his head; fighting all those demons and everything bad that had happened to him; whatever those things were. I had to remind myself that there was nothing wrong with me.

———

I AWOKE WITH A START, dropping the empty wine glass onto the carpet. The house was dark. A car drove past, its lights shining through the gap in the curtains, blinding me. I rubbed my eyes. I shivered. The hair on the back of my neck stood on end. My spine stiffened, and I glanced around. Nothing. The fridge made a noise and then went back to its usual humming. The microwave flashed the time; 19:38. I couldn't believe I'd slept for so long.

I picked up the glass and padded barefoot to the kitchen, switching on the light. I cringed when I felt something beneath my foot. Raising my leg to see, noticing a purple powder. My skin crawled. The cork from the bottle was still on the counter and had some of the same purple powder on the edges. I licked dry lips, wishing I had a glass of water. Nearing the counter, I stuck my finger into the mouth of the bottle, and some of the powder came out with it. I washed my hands quickly and drank water from the faucet.

Something didn't feel right; my vision was blurry, and muscles felt weak. Slowly, I traversed up the stairs and entered my bedroom. The light was on; I could've sworn it was off when I left this morning. I used the toilet in my ensuite bathroom, and the smell of an unknown perfume wafted in the air.

I entered my room again, and she stood with a knife in her hand, glowering at me.

Chapter Thirty-Three

DANA

MOM'S HOUSE? I thought after reading Pam's message. She was at her mom's place. I knew where that was and made a note. I'd been so busy I hadn't finished looking into Julia McBride. Her DMV photo popped up, making me squint. She had brown hair, no makeup, and she seemed almost boring looking; the opposite of what she looked like now. I tilted my head to the side; she reminded me of someone.

I inserted her name into the search engine and pages full of results for me to choose from. I opened the first page's links into various tabs and went into each one.

The first tab was her wedding to a rich man ten years ago; he was at least thirty years older than her. I stared at his face, noticing a darkness in his features as he held her possessively by her neck in each picture. The look in Julia's eyes told me she wasn't happy to be there, and I couldn't help but wonder if it was an arranged marriage or one of convenience. Now I understood her having an affair with Ethan.

The second tab was from her Instagram account; it was a collage of food photos, restaurants she ate at, countries she visited. Everything made her look happy and spoiled and living her best life.

The third tab made me flinch. Her Facebook account with a photo of her standing beside her younger sister; a woman I recognized. Although she was younger and thinner, I couldn't miss that sweet innocent face that belonged to Beverly. Something told me there was more to Julia, that perhaps she helped avenge her sister's abuser.

I had to tell Donnie and James and called my brother.

"Yoh," he said.

"Donnie, it's Julia."

"What do you mean?"

"Julia is Beverly's sister. Julia is the killer."

"How do you know about Beverly?"

Dammit. I had to come clean again. "I saw the police file when James brought it home last night."

"I can't believe you did that. Did you know what your wife did?" Donnie asked James.

"You can moan at me later," I said, even though I knew it was a good thing I did; otherwise, they'd realize this too late. "Maybe she and Ethan worked together, or she did this on her own; you need to question both of them again." Pausing for a moment, I let it sink in. "You need to do that today, like now."

"Why?"

"Bad feeling," I said, thinking about Pam's message. "And Pam is at her mom's house in Oak Brook."

"Okay," Donnie said, mumbling something to James. *"We'll contact them now, hear where Julia and Ethan are."*

"Donnie?"

"Yeah?"

"I'm going to see if Pam's okay."

Chapter Thirty-Four

PAM

"JULIA?" I said, stepping closer to the door for an easy exit, but she was blocking my way. "What are you doing here?"

"You know, Pam," Julia said menacingly. "I wouldn't have bothered coming here if you hadn't followed us to your house. I mean, you watched us sleep like some pervert, and still had the audacity to hold a knife as if you would ever use it. You're too weak, too pathetic, someone I could crush with the heel of my shoe."

I raised my hands, taken aback. "Why Julia?" I asked, glancing around, trying to find a way out. "Why do you want to hurt me? You can have Ethan. I definitely don't want him anymore."

"But you're going to blame him for Tom's death and take him away from me. Then you're going to take half his assets, which belong to *me*." She poked at her chest with her index finger.

"Why though? Your husband is rich with one foot in the grave."

She shook her head. "He kicked me out, leaving me

with nothing. You know me, Pam, I can't have nothing. I need it all, and I need Ethan to give it to me."

It wasn't love; she was only using Ethan. And Ethan was using her; they deserved each other. I hoped karma tended to them soon.

"Did you kill Tom?" I asked.

The sinister grin splitting her face in two left me horrified, making me wonder if she enjoyed killing Tom.

"Why?" I asked with a shrug. "We could've worked things out during the divorce. Nobody had to die."

"You know what Tom did to all those girls," Julia said, gesturing with the knife. "He did those horrible things to my sister Beverly. She changed so much after that night. Thank goodness she has a family with two beautiful children, but she's still traumatized after all these years. Tom was a bad person, and I can't believe you fell for him. How stupid are you?"

My throat ached as I fought back tears. "Your sister fell for him. I fell for him. So many women fell for him. It doesn't mean there's anything wrong with us. He was not a nice guy, Julia. That doesn't mean you have to kill me." My eyes flitted from her face to the knife in her hand.

"Of course it does," Ethan said, entering the room.

I stepped backwards, hitting the bathroom door frame with my back. I held onto that frame in case I needed to dash into the bathroom and lock myself inside.

"Why, Ethan?" I asked, hating the desperation in my voice.

"I've wanted out of our marriage for a long time, but that prenup you made me sign stopped me from doing it. Then I met Julia." He glanced lovingly at her. "You see, Pam, it's always about the money. How do you not understand this?" he asked sarcastically. "I can't have you take half. Then, when Julia told me about Tom and the awful things he did to her sister and so many other women, I thought I might as well kill two birds with one stone."

Julia laughed. "I wanted to kill you too, but then I told Ethan to wait, let the cops blame you and arrest you instead. I mean, isn't that the perfect murder?"

Ethan stepped closer to Julia, waving an even bigger knife in my direction. "I hate to admit it, but it was kind of cool watching him bleed." The smile creeping up Ethan's face left me horrified. I'd never seen this side of him; I never knew he even had such a dark side, and I couldn't help but wonder who was worse; Ethan or Tom?

"I couldn't agree more, honey." She leaned over and kissed him chastely. "What are we going to do about her? You know we can't leave her like this." She wielded the knife in my direction.

"We need the police off our backs," he said. His tone ominous. I'd never heard him sound like that before; he was not the Ethan I'd married. "We need to kill her. She's already swallowed enough pills to make them believe she did this to herself." Then he turned towards me. "Run a bath."

Chapter Thirty-Five

DANA

I ARRIVED at Pam's mom's house sooner than I thought and parked near the neighbor's house; I didn't want to alert anyone inside that I was here. All the lights were off except in the bedroom on the second floor. The silhouettes of two people moved in front of the drawn curtains by the window. My phone vibrated.

"They're gone. We're on our way. Do nothing stupid," Donnie wrote.

"They're here! Hurry! I'm going in."

Donnie phoned, but I cancelled the call and ran across the lawn towards the front door. Slowly, I tried the door handle; it opened quietly. Once inside, I heard three voices; two female, one male. Carefully, I traversed up the stairs with my weapon raised. They were in the main bedroom.

"Fill the tub," Ethan yelled.

I crouched and crept towards the bedroom door, and was careful they didn't see me when I glanced inside.

"She's ready," Julia called.

I entered the bedroom when I was sure they were all in the bathroom.

"Do I cut her wrists like this or like that?" Julia asked. Her voice echoing.

"Down her arm," Ethan said.

"You don't have to do this," Pam cried.

I moved closer. All three were in the bathroom, hovering over Pam in the bath. She crossed her arms over her chest so they couldn't get to her.

"Give me your arms," Julia demanded, sounding like a spoiled child.

"Step away from her," I said, aiming my weapon at Julia and then at Ethan.

Ethan spun around, pointing his knife at me. He moved in front of Julia.

"Move to the side," I yelled, motioning with my gun where he needed to stand.

"You can't be here," he said, sure of himself.

"Really?" I said sarcastically. "You two are committing a crime. Now step away from her. Pam, get out of the tub and take Julia's knife away."

"Don't touch me," Julia said, holding onto Ethan's waist.

Still clothed, Pam climbed out of the bath and dried herself as best she could.

"You can't touch us." Ethan's tone was serious, and I wondered if he was delusional. They were committing a crime, but he thought I couldn't have them arrested.

"The police are on their way," I said.

He shrugged nonchalantly.

"Come here, Pam," I said, still aiming my weapon at Ethan.

As Pam passed Ethan and Julia, Julia lunged for her. I pulled the trigger; the bullet hitting Julia in the shoulder.

Ethan dove for me, screaming like a maniac. As I turned to fire, he slammed into me and we flew backwards. We landed on the carpet hard. Julia cried somewhere in the bathroom. Pam jumped onto Ethan's back, getting him off me. He hit me in the face and then smacked the gun out of my hands. I moaned; the hit to my head from crashing to the floor with a grown man on top of me was too much, and I tried to suck air back in my lungs.

"Get off me," Ethan groaned, gripping Pam's wrists and yanking her off him and to the side, but she held onto him, taking him with her.

I pushed farther away from them and reached for my gun.

Sirens wailed in the background.

Relief washed over me knowing Donnie and James were on their way. My diaphragm ached as I breathed. I grabbed my gun. The police broke open the front door. Heavy footsteps up the stairs. And before I aimed my gun at Ethan, Donnie and James had him in handcuffs.

Chapter Thirty-Six

DANA

I SAT on the ambulance bed beside Pam, who was being stitched up. Julia had cut Pam on her arm but luckily not too deep.

Donnie and James hovered around us taking our statement.

"I think that's it," Donnie said, closing his notebook.

"Did you know about Julia's sister?" I asked Pam.

She nodded. "She came with Julia to the gym one day, but she was skittish and left soon after arriving. When I saw Julia the next day, she explained Beverly had gone through something traumatic and something triggered her. If I'd known she recognized Tom, then maybe I could've helped, but what bothers me is Julia said nothing when Tom and I got closer. She didn't warn me; she claimed to be my friend yet said nothing."

"I think it's because she wanted your husband and you out of the way," I said. "Perhaps she wanted Tom to hurt you like he hurt her sister, then when she found out Tom had fallen in love with you, it made her bitter. You were the one who *changed* him," I added, thinking out loud.

"Hmm, maybe," she said, flinching when the paramedic added the last stitch.

"There, all done," the paramedic said. "Will both of you ladies be coming to the hospital?"

"No," we said at the same time.

"I'm going home," Pam said, standing. "I've had enough thrills to last me a lifetime. I want to go home and see my kids."

"They're with your neighbors," Donnie said matter-of-factly.

"Thanks," she said with tears in her eyes.

"Come," I said, standing and jumping out of the ambulance. "I'll take you home."

"What about my mom's house?" Pam stared at the broken front door."

"Don't worry," I said, pulling her into a sideways hug. "They'll put the door back." I glanced at Donnie, arching my eyebrows.

"That's right," Donnie said, elbowing my side. "The house is safe."

Donnie and James made way for us, walking us to my car. A police cruiser drove past with Ethan in the back.

"Where are they taking him?" Pam asked.

"We need to question him," James said, leaning against my car with his arms folded across his chest. "We need to understand what happened that night and who killed Tom."

"They'll probably blame each other," Pam said.

"I think it was Julia," I said, opening my car door.

———

THE MOMENT PAM climbed into my car and glanced at me, she burst into tears. "Sorry," she said. The more tears she wiped away, the more she cried.

"Don't be. You've gone through something very traumatic, and the person you loved tried to kill you. Cry all you need to." I handed her tissues from my handbag.

"Thanks," she said. "I don't want the kids to see me crying."

"Maybe they need to see you cry," I added. "They need to know how bad it was."

"I don't know what to tell them."

"You'll figure it out."

She cried the entire way. When we stopped outside her house, her face was dry; it was just her eyes that were still red and puffy.

There were police cruisers in her driveway, and the kids were inside with two adults and two policewomen.

"Are they your neighbors?"

"Yes, the Hendricks," Pam said, opening the car door when I turned off the ignition.

"Mom!" the kids yelled, seeing us through the window and running outside to greet her. It was such an emotional reunion. Crying in the car helped little because Pam cried as she hugged her kids. There was a cacophony of questions from them. The most serious one was, where was their father now?

The police officers left along with the Hendricks, leaving mom and kids to speak in private. I stood outside and watched, smiling and relieved things ended the way they did. My friend was no longer in danger, and the culprits would soon be behind bars.

As I turned to leave, Pam called me back, running towards me and hugging me. "Thank you for believing in me," she said tearfully. "Thank you for helping me. And thank you for everything. I wouldn't have been able to do this without you."

"It's my pleasure," I said, giving her one last squeeze before letting go. "I'm glad it all worked out."

"It's a good thing you found the Body Count book and connected all the dots."

"Me too. Have a good evening now that you're back home with the kids."

"Thanks," she said, smiling. "It feels good to be home." Her smiled widened. "Thanks again."

Donnie and James would be at the station for a long time questioning the two suspects, and I wanted to get home, make dinner and enjoy a glass of wine. The day had been long and filled with plenty of action; now it was time to rest.

Chapter Thirty-Seven

DONNIE

"WERE you the one who cut Tom?" I asked.

Julia shifted in her chair. Her perfectly styled hair had fallen flat against her head and was now tied in a high ponytail with wisps framing her face. Her makeup had smudged, and her face had paled. Nobody looked great in their mugshot, and she was no different, being charged with murder and attempted murder changed everyone.

She leaned back in her chair contemptuously, folding her arms across her chest. The flesh wound to her shoulder neatly bandaged. The lawyer beside her kept quiet.

"Ethan is going to pin everything on you. Why don't you tell us your side of the story first?" James added.

She sighed loudly, rolling her eyes into the back of her head. "You know what kind of man Tom was, why do you need me to spell it out?" She shouted and then clucked her tongue.

"We need to know everything that happened that night. Please tell us your version," I said.

She glanced at her lawyer, who nodded. "I didn't know

Tom was *the* Tom who'd hurt Beverly. It angered me he worked with women and continued doing his wicked deeds. When Ethan and I started our affair and Pam was drooling all over Tom, I thought it was the perfect plan; he'd do to her what he did to others and it would leave her a mess and she would never know about me and Ethan and she wouldn't care about the divorce because she would be too busy nursing her wounds."

She was a piece of work; I gave her credit for that. And selfish. Incredibly selfish woman. "Go on," I said.

"But Ethan wanted Pam out of our lives for good and came up with a plan to use those same drugs on them."

"How did Ethan know about the drugs Tom used?"

"Lucky," she said. "Lucky said he'd give Ethan the drugs Tom used on the women, but we didn't know how to give them to Tom. So Lucky offered to do it for us."

I glanced at James, who nodded. We needed to bring Lucky to the station for questioning. James excused himself and made the call for one of our officers to go pick him up.

"Did you tell Lucky why you wanted Tom to have the drugs? Did he know your plans?"

"Nah, we didn't give him details, just said we wanted him to have the same experience he gave the women."

"And then what?" I said, glancing up at the camera recording everything.

"We waited. We watched them at the club, and then when they were ready to leave, we followed them. Tom was completely out of it yet managed to drive carefully and got them to his apartment safely. He didn't lock his front door, so we entered and waited for them to fall asleep. But they didn't just fall asleep. The guy had sex with Pam that lasted two hours; he's an animal. I've never seen someone fuck as hard as he did." She shook her head. "I mean, it was sexy as hell, but still, we wanted to kill him and get out of there. Anyway, like most men, after he came, he started snoring. Tom was as strong as an elephant, and Ethan had to keep him down while he cut him first, then I cut down, so that it was deeper, and then I opened the wound to see inside his neck. It was so gross, but I was glad we did that."

It explained why there were two different lacerations, making both accused murderers. They'd be going away for a long time.

"So yeah, it wasn't just Ethan, and it wasn't just me; it was both of us. We wanted Pam dead as well, but then thought the cops would think she did it, and I left my knife under her pillow after I left her fingerprints on the handle."

Julia played with her handcuffs, not looking at me while she recounted the events. I excused myself and went to the interview room next door, where Ethan sat with his lawyer and a permanent scowl stuck on his face.

"Julia explained what happened that evening," I said, sitting down. The door opened, and James entered, sitting beside me. He nodded, silently confirming that Lucky was on his way.

Ethan continued giving us his death stare.

"We'll be charging you both for the murder of Tom and attempted murder of Pamela—"

"You have no proof," Ethan yelled, slamming his fists on the table. His lawyer grabbed his arm, pulling him to one side to whisper in his ear. "My alibi shows I was at a work function," he said calmly.

"See, that's where your ego got ahead of you." I pulled the pages out of the file to show them. "We asked for proof that it was you at the conference, and the picture sent to us was of a man looking nothing like you. Tell me, how much did it cost to hire an actor to stand in for you?"

Ethan pursed his lips, and his face reddened. His lawyer's jaw dropped open; he clearly didn't know how imaginative his client truly was.

"And right now your prints are being compared to those found at the scene. It looks like you may have missed a few places where you touched."

Ethan's nostrils flared, and his jaw ticked.

"Tell us your side," I said, opening my notepad and clicking my pen.

"Go ahead, tell them everything," his lawyer said. "If you cooperate, they won't hit you with everything."

I nodded my thanks to the lawyer; for once, they weren't making things worse.

Ethan sighed. "Pam and I had drifted apart. It was years in the making and not something that happened suddenly. When I met Julia, she woke something inside of me, and I couldn't let that slip away; I needed to find out if it was something real. We met again, and from then on, we couldn't keep our hands off each other. She told me about her awful husband, who controlled everything and said if she ever divorced him, he'd leave her with nothing even though their prenup stated she'd receive a percentage. That's when I remembered my prenup, which left me angry at Pam forcing me to sign that thing; I couldn't afford to give her half. I wanted her gone but not dead and didn't know how to do it."

Ethan sipped on his water, then continued, "When Julia found out Tom liked Pam, but it was also the same Tom who'd hurt her sister, I started digging, needing to find out how Tom went about doing these things so that I could replicate it and have Pam blamed for his murder. I approached his drug dealer to find out everything. I paid him a lot of money for this information and for the pills.

And when Lucky offered to swap the good pills with the bad, I accepted." He shrugged nonchalantly. "I guess things would've gone according to plan if her friend hadn't butted in."

———

"WHAT AN ASSHOLE," James said as we neared the coffee station.

"Yeah, a real piece of work," I said, stirring sugar in my coffee.

"Is Lucky here?" James asked an officer who usually worked at the front desk.

"Someone arrived and has been sitting in interview room four."

"Thanks," James said, wiggling his eyebrows. "Now it's Lucky's turn to come clean."

Lucky looked worse than the last time we interviewed him. He hadn't brushed his dark curly hair, and some strands had knotted. His red beard looked scratchy, bushy eyebrows raised, and his red-rimmed eyes seemed vacant. His addiction had become his enemy.

"How are you doing?" I asked.

Lucky glanced at me with pain in his eyes. He fidgeted with his fingers. He'd bitten his nails down to the nub, and some had dried blood. "I've been better, Detective."

"Why is that?"

"My friend is dead." He blinked unshed tears.

"Do you think you may have caused that?"

He stared straight ahead, then finally nodded.

"I need to hear you say it, Lucky."

"Yes, okay," he shouted, "I think I'm the cause."

"Did you and Tom have an altercation at his gym?"

Lucky glanced at me. "How did you know?"

"His manager saw it happen and confirmed when we showed him a picture of you. What did you argue about?"

"I wanted a job; I'd been to other places, but I have a record, you know. I wanted to get out of this business, but Tom didn't want to help me. He said I was a nobody, a nothing, and could never do what he did. He thought he was better than me because he made more money, his muscles were bigger than mine, and women still fell at his feet. I told him I didn't care, and he had to make a plan; I'd even clean the bathrooms. I had to get out of this man; it's busy killing me." Lucky's voice broke towards the end.

"Is that why you agreed with Ethan to give Tom his special drugs?"

Lucky nodded.

"You need to say it, Lucky."

"Yes, okay, I was angry at Tom for being a fucking dick towards me. I hated what he did to the women. I hated him for using everyone. And when he wouldn't help me, I wanted him dead. I wanted him to pay for something. Karma was taking too long with that dude, man. Now look, he's finally dead because of me, and I still feel like shit. Still in this shitty mess I created, and I have nobody to blame but myself." Lucky rubbed his tired face. He snorted hard and swallowed. I shuddered; it was gross.

"Who supplied you with all the pills?" I asked.

He averted his eyes, staring at a spot in the corner.

"Lucky," I said, wanting him to look at me. When he did, I continued, "Give us his name. Who makes these drugs? We need details."

"He's a tough motherfucker, and if he knows I said anything, he'll kill me."

"Give us something and we'll do our own investigation, leaving you out of it."

"What about Tom's death?"

"We'll still charge you, but if you help us, we might reduce your sentence." I didn't know if that was possible, just as long as we got answers.

Chapter Thirty-Eight

DONNIE

WITH JULIA, Ethan, and Lucky in jail, all we needed now was to arrest Miguel; the pharmacist who made his own recreational drugs while Lucky and Tom sold them for him. According to Lucky, when Tom asked Miguel to make something *special* for him, he didn't hesitate. Now, we needed to understand how it all unfolded.

Lucky gave us the drugs he had leftover, and on each of them was the logo of Miguel's pharmacy; a big *'M'*. Not the smartest thing to do, it's as if Miguel wanted recognition for his drugs without the accountability. We put in an urgent request to have the pills tested, and Dr. Warryn confirmed it had the same chemical makeup as the traces found in Tom's blood.

We knew Miguel was at home and had a secret cellar where he made the drugs. The SWAT team descended upon his property in a flash, getting him out of his cellar in handcuffs. The shocked expression on his face told me he thought he'd never get caught.

Once SWAT had taken him away, and they had checked his residence, we entered.

Miguel had left the grass to grow tall, with weeds sprouting sporadically. There were old tires in one corner with the tall grass covering them, sun-damaged toys, a broken bucket, and even old clothing strewn about.

We went to the shed first. It looked normal with rakes, a lawnmower, and tools, but the trapdoor in the floor opened to a sterile room that told us more about Miguel as a man than anything we'd find in his house.

It was a large, white room with metal workbenches, beakers, flasks, and everything a chemist would need to make drugs. It reminded me of the series *Breaking Bad*. The room smelled of chemicals even though we wore masks. Our gloves weren't very thick, and they'd warned us not to touch any of the chemicals until they tested everything for safety. Miguel could've been working on something far more dangerous than a date rape drug.

In one corner, there was a recliner chair in front of a television with VHS tapes. I pushed a tape in and switched the television on. A grainy film started; it looked like a cheap porn movie until I recognized Tom.

"Jeez," James said, stepping closer. "He did record everything."

"Maybe this was how Tom paid for the pills." I opened the TV cabinet drawer and there were rows and rows of tapes. "I hate being the one going through all this crap."

"I wonder if there's more than one girl per tape?"

"And there's nothing written on it," I said, standing. I stopped the tape when Tom approached a sleeping woman on a bed. "Just looking at this for five seconds can leave a stain on you."

"Yeah," James said with a shudder. "Just as long as I'm not the one going through all of them."

The lab technicians entered the room in their hazmat suits and started testing the chemicals before removing them.

"Let's give them the room and go to the house," James said, heading for the ladder.

Miguel's home reminded me of those from the sixties; the decor frozen in time. We entered the kitchen first and strolled through each room as the crime scene technicians collected evidence.

"Let's check out his room," James said, entering the larger of the two bedrooms.

It didn't look like he'd made his bed in a while, with a crusty substance between the sheet and blanket. There was clothing on the floor and dirty underwear on the chest of drawers.

"Don't forget to process those," I said to the closest technician, pointing at the undies.

"Why, you wanna take them home afterwards," he said, chuckling.

"I'll pass, but thanks," I said, laughing. "This guy is gross. I mean, look at this." I pointed at all the dirty clothes strewn everywhere. "It's like he never cleaned and didn't know what to wear."

"Huge contrast comparing his room to his cellar," James said, peering into the ensuite bathroom.

"Yeah," I said, following him to the bathroom. There was grime on the tiles, in the shower, and around the bath. "Just gross. It doesn't look like he showered much."

The next room was the study. Shelves lined one wall filled with books. There was a large wooden desk and an old leather chair behind it. We searched the drawers, finding folders and not much else. I moved the mouse, and the computer screen lit up; not password protected.

"When last did that happen?" I asked, sitting behind the desk, and searched for anything strange on the computer.

"Maybe he has nothing to hide."

"Or maybe he wants to get caught," I said. In all the years I'd been a cop, had a suspect not password protect their computer.

I went to the *Trash* folder first, finding lots of deleted photos. I highlighted them all and clicked on *Recover*. In the photos folder, I found pictures of all the women Tom had drugged. "Makes me sick," I mumbled to myself.

"What did you find?" James asked, standing behind me.

I turned the screen so he could see and continue clicking through all the photos, stopping at one that was different. "Please tell me that's not what I think it is?"

"Under eighteen, or rather under sixteen. It's disgusting," James said with a sigh and walked away. "Get violent crimes to look into that so we can add child pornography to his list of charges."

I browsed quickly through the pictures, finding more and more underage children. "Tom's not in any of these. I think it's Miguel's private stash; possibly took the pictures himself or part of a wider network." Finding something like this didn't happen often, so it was a bit of a shock to my system, and based on James's reaction, he wasn't too happy either. It's never a good feeling to see these things, but it relieved me that Miguel was already in custody. Now, all we had to figure out who belonged in his network.

James shook his head and continued searching the filing cabinet. "Oh no," he said, pulling out a large see-through bag.

"What?" I stood to see what he was going on about. "What are those?" My eyes narrowed.

"Tom's victim's mementos. Panties, licenses, bras, jewelry, and even a purse."

"Why does Miguel have them?"

"Who knows," James said, placing the bag on the floor and checking the cabinet one last time before opening the next drawer. "Here are the patient files." He browsed through them. "Miguel had information about the women. What they're allergic to, what chronic medication they were on, if they were on birth control."

"Were they patients at his pharmacy?"

"Must be. It's possible he needed their information so that the drugs he made wouldn't cause adverse reactions." He pulled out a flyer. "There's also a stack of ads for parties at the warehouse. Miguel must've had this at the pharmacy, then when the women came in they'd see the flyer and go to the warehouse where Tom would pick them up. He already knew the mark before meeting them."

"Christ," I said, shocked by this. It's like they had an entire system for finding victims. "I wonder what else they took from the ladies?" I asked.

———

MIGUEL'S FACE was full of hard, angry lines. His straight dark hair was in his face, covering intelligent eyes. At first glance, he came across as someone who didn't know any better, but that's how he fooled people. He knew what he was doing.

He declined to have a lawyer present. We'd see if he spoke to us.

"Miguel, do you understand why we arrested you?" I asked as James sat beside me.

"You found some things after illegally searching my property."

"No, the search was legal." I placed printouts of the photos of the naked girls in front of him. "These we found on your home computer, along with these." I placed the items we'd found in the bag in his study on the table near his hands. He didn't look at any of the items. "We also found your patient files, and the movies Tom made for you. We can connect the women in the Body Count book to the VHS tapes and to these mementos Tom gave you. You're just as guilty of raping those women as Tom is. Oh, and you made the illegal drugs. You'll be going away for a very long time, Mr. Perez."

We had more than enough evidence connecting him to the crimes, but it would be interesting to hear his side of the story, if he said anything.

One side of Miguel's lips twitched upward as if he knew something we didn't. "It took you long enough," he said.

"Did you want to get caught?" I asked.

He pursed his lips but his eyes smiled. I took that as a 'yes'.

"I find it amazing that you have all this but can't see what's in front of you," Miguel said.

"Yeah?" I said, leaning my elbows on the table. "What's that?"

"None of this would've been possible if it weren't for the parties at the warehouse."

Chapter Thirty-Nine

DONNIE

THIS CASE WAS BECOMING INTERTWINED as we discovered more people were involved in illegal activity. First it was Tom, Lucky, then Miguel, and now Ben. Everybody played a part in Tom's dark fantasy; each was guilty in their own way.

Once we had the warrant, we headed over to the warehouse. Everyone was busy doing something as they got the party ready for this evening. Ben rushed over to us demanding that we leave.

"We have a warrant to search the place," I said, handing him the papers.

"What? Why?" Ben asked, paling, and taking it from me. "What are you searching for?"

"Narcotics, weapons, photos. We want anything and everything," I said, surveying the area. "Everybody out!" I yelled, watching the staff scurry outside, "and don't leave the premises." I pointed at a barman running for the exit, who then slowed to a walk.

Officers began searching every dark corner. James and I

were heading for Ben's office when shouts erupted about something being found. We hurried over to the utility closet. Two officers held up bags of recreational pills; the purple ones with Miguel's logo.

"Where did you find that?" I asked.

"Under the metal shelf," the officer holding the bags said.

"He's getting away!" Another officer yelled.

We spun around and ran after Ben. The same officer who'd yelled was ahead of us, slamming his body into Ben's, sending them both into the wall near the exit. Ben crumpled to the floor like a rag doll, out cold.

"Are you okay?" I asked the officer, who stood nodding. "Great job."

"Thanks, Detective." He doubled over, sucking in deep breaths of air.

Ben mumbled on the floor, slowly coming to and sitting up.

"So…" I left my word hanging. "Anything you'd like to tell us? Someone else you want to blame?"

"Detective," another officer said, holding a smaller bag also belonging to Miguel, but the pills were dark purple. "We found these in his office."

Ben leered at me.

"Why are these different?" I asked, holding up the bag and then giving it back to the officer. "Are you also using Tom's special stash?"

Ben pursed his lips, averting his eyes.

"Handcuff him and take him down to the station. I want to have a look around before heading back and questioning him," I told the officer who'd slammed into Ben. "Let's go," I said to James.

Ben's office had metal cabinets, a wooden desk, and a

leather chair held together with duct tape. The officer who found the pills continued the search while we helped.

"Anything else?" I asked him.

"Not yet, Detective."

James sat behind the old wooden desk and rummaged through the drawers. He pulled out folders and stacks of papers from the desk.

"Wait," I said, pointing, "what's that?"

James pushed papers out of the way, revealing photos of naked women and underage girls. "Seems he was collecting them, too."

"I wonder if Miguel and Ben are part of the same network?" I asked, feeling nauseous and not wanting to look at any of the photos.

"Well, they knew each other, and I recognize some girls." He tapped the photo. "Maybe they share these with others."

"I hope they're all put away for a very long time."

"We have enough evidence," James said, dropping the photos in an evidence bag. "I don't think there's anything else here. Seems we found what we wanted."

"Yeah," I said, relieved, but not as ecstatic as I'd hoped. Finding these photos in Ben's office told me how sick he was, too. It's like a disease that, once it found someone else with a similar disposition, it could easily spread. "I hope that's all of them now."

Chapter Forty

DANA

I WAITED PATIENTLY for James to get home. He'd been working non-stop since yesterday. He messaged me an hour ago that he was on his way home.

I read the sentence three times before I understood what was going on in the book and turned the page. I'd probably need to read *The Last Girl* by Natalie Michaels again because the suspense of what happened in the case was killing me, but my mind kept wandering.

I flinched when the door opened and bolted towards James. "You're home!" I wrapped my arms around his neck, kissing him chastely.

"Hey," he said, kissing me again. "Were you waiting for me just so you could do that?" He asked with a smirk.

"Oh yes, absolutely, you know me so well." My smile reached my eyes. "Okay, tell me what happened. Leave nothing out."

He chuckled, shaking his head. "Coffee first."

We sat in the lounge drinking our coffee. James wore a bright smile, but his eyes were tired from working two days on little sleep. "Our violent crimes unit will investigate the child pornography we found at Miguel's home and Ben's office."

"I still can't believe that," I said, shocked at what they'd found. I never would've guessed they were like that, but then again, I didn't know these men at all. Come to think of it, they made my skin crawl. And to think Lucky had lied to my face about what he'd done; he was a junky and a dealer, I shouldn't have expected honesty from someone like him. Perhaps Lucky telling me about the Body Count book and Ethan buying pills from him was a way of owning up to what he'd done. Maybe. I didn't question him, so I'd never know. Everything about this case shocked me.

"I know. One good thing coming out of Pam's horrific ordeal is we're taking these two men off the streets. I can only hope we'll find more guys behind the dark web who shared these pictures."

I didn't like these types of investigations. The people working in the violent crime unit had to have hearts made of stone and an even stronger stomach. Not forgetting the hackers who helped search for the pedophiles. It was a job for the toughest men and women.

"I'm just glad it worked out for Pam," I said with a sigh. "She's home with the kids and her killer husband behind bars." I finished my coffee and raised my legs to place them on James's lap. I wiggled my toes. He grinned, setting his mug down and started rubbing my feet.

"It sounds like he'll be going away for a long time too. Do you think she'll get a job now that he's gone?" He asked, pressing hard on my left big toe.

"She has to," I said through gritted teeth. The massage was wonderful, but it hurt; James was pressing on all the sore pressure points. "Or maybe her mom will help, unless Ethan had policies she can cash."

"And the violent crime unit is looking into Tom's Body Count book to account for all the women in there."

"Good," I said. "What he did is awful." It would haunt me knowing the guy I liked did something so terrible to so many women. Tom got what he deserved in the end, even though Pam didn't deserve any of the stress. I felt sorry for Pam; she fell in love with a man who had a dark past. And I doubted anyone could live with themselves staying with a partner like Tom. I hoped Pam still believed in love and found someone who knew how to take care of her.

Chapter Forty-One

DONNIE

"THANK YOU FOR STOPPING BY," Dr. Warryn said, pulling out an evidence bag. "The dark cherry lipstick you found under the bed had traces of Atropa Bella-donna, otherwise known as deadly nightshade."

"Really?" I asked, my interest piqued. "Surely the date rape drug he'd ingested along with the deadly nightshade would've killed him?"

"He's tough, but no, the quantities weren't large enough to kill him."

"Did he kiss someone with the lipstick on?" I asked. "But surely the lipstick would've poisoned the other person too"

"Your assumptions are correct," Dr Warryn said. "But no, he kissed no one wearing the lipstick. I found some of the lipstick inside Tom's mouth," he added, pointing to the inside of his cheek. "Deadly nightshade contains atropine and scopolamine, so the quantities we found wasn't enough to kill him, just incapacitated him."

I glanced at James, who shrugged. "I wonder who it belonged to."

"There were no fingerprints on the lipstick."

"Do you think Julia gave it to him to make killing him easier?" James asked.

"Maybe you'll have to ask her," Dr. Warryn said. "Pam's DNA matched the blood found in Tom's kitchen and shower." He continued reading from his report. "Oh, and we found no other secret compartments in Tom's apartment, but we found hidden cameras for all those videos he filmed."

"Okay," I said, getting ready to leave. "Thanks for the update."

On our way back to the station, we arranged to question Julia again, and she was waiting for us in an interview room when we arrived. Her hair was oily and in a messy ponytail. There were bags under her red-rimmed eyes, and she kept tugging at the unflattering inmate jumpsuit she wore.

"Thank you for meeting us without your lawyer," I said, sitting down.

"None of it matters anyway," she said nonchalantly.

"Does this belong to you?" I asked, placing the bagged lipstick in front of her.

She shook her head. "Nah, man, not my color."

"Are you sure you've never seen it?"

"Yeah, never. I don't wear that color. I'm more of a nude type of girl."

"Do you think it's Pam's?" James asked as we exited the station.

"If it's not Julia's, it must be Pam's then. But it makes little sense," I said, opening my car door. "Why would she give it to Tom? She's been adamant she had nothing to do with his death even though she was the only one with him before Ethan and Julia arrived. And if Dr. Warryn is correct, Tom ingested it before he died, so whoever gave it to him was in the room."

"And we have no way of knowing if Pam had brought it with her."

We arrived at Pam's home. James knocked. After the third knock, she opened the door. "Detectives? Is everything okay?" She asked with wide eyes.

"We just have a few questions to ask you before we wrap this up."

"Sure, come on in."

We entered her house, following her up a step and into the living room. There were family pictures on the mantelpiece, a couple of individual pictures of each child, Ethan and Pamela together, and a black-and-white picture of a young girl I didn't recognize. We'd been inside their home once before when we asked Ethan for some hair that belonged to Pamela, but it was the first time I noticed the people in the photos.

"We won't take long," James said. "How are you doing now that you're back home?"

"Good," she said, beaming. "Glad to be home with my kids. Relieved everything is over. Well, after the trial it will be over."

James raised the lipstick in a see-through evidence bag. "Do you recognize this?"

She frowned and squinted. "No," she said, wanting to take the bag from him but didn't. "Never. I don't wear lipstick. Where did you find it?"

"Under Tom's bed. There were traces found in his mouth before he died."

"Sorry, I remember nothing about that night after we

took those two pills. I wish I could remember more." She tilted her head to the side; she seemed lost in thought.

"Can you remember anyone else coming to speak to either you or Ethan while you were still at the club?"

"No, not that I can recall. The only other person I spoke to was Dana, and then I think I saw you there but am not sure. I was hallucinating quite a bit." She raised a shoulder and blushed. "It was the first time I'd taken anything like that. I wish I didn't." She sighed wearily.

I believed her. We didn't know what Tom did or how he got the lipstick inside his mouth, and we didn't really know what Julia did no matter what she told us. I was curious about something, though. "Who is that?" I asked, pointing at the black-and-white photo.

Pamela glanced at the photo. "That's Ethan's younger sister. She passed away a few years ago. Her passing devastated the family, as you can imagine. Everyone had such high hopes for her."

"What happened?"

"She killed herself about ten years ago." Pam picked up the photo frame and stared at it for a while, then placed it neatly back on the mantelpiece. "If I remember correctly, she wore lipstick almost that color." She pointed at the lipstick in James's hand.

"Do you know why she killed herself?" I asked.

"I don't think anyone knows. She didn't leave a note behind, nothing. She swallowed some poison and drifted off to sleep in her bed."

I glanced at James, who arched an eyebrow. "Would that poison be Deadly Nightshade?"

"I don't know; it could be. You'd have to ask Ethan. He didn't share all the details with me at the time of her death. It devastated him more than anyone else in the family. They were very close. After her death, it's as if a part of him died as well."

Back at the station, James and I went through the Body Count book. I'd taken a picture of Ethan's sister, Candace, to see if we could find her. James opened the book to the first page, and there she was; Tom's first victim.

I could tell Candace wasn't all there by how Tom kept her upright. And the lipstick could be the same shade.

"This happened about twelve years ago," James said. "I wonder if Candace told Ethan what Tom had done to her?"

"She must've otherwise how would he know about the lipstick." I pointed at the picture.

"We'll need to speak with him again," James said, standing and stretching out his back. "We need to tie up this loose end and get Ethan's statement."

———

ETHAN STARED daggers at me and then at James. Anger radiated off him in waves, making my arms pebble. It seemed he hated everyone because of the things he did in life.

James opened the Body Count book to the first page. Ethan didn't look at it. Then James held the lipstick high enough for him to see it, but he stared past it.

"We know you laced the lipstick with Deadly Night-shade," I said, flicking the pen open and closed.

The noise of the pen clicking caught his attention, and he turned his dark gaze on me, one side of his mouth curved upward.

"You wanted to make sure Tom couldn't hurt anyone again, so you used the same poison your sister took to kill herself on him." During our investigation, we'd found out that Candace cultivated nootropics and had started tinkering with dangerous plants as an alternative to supplements to improve thinking, learning, and memory. Death by deadly nightshade was relatively quick, but Candace had masked her poison in her lipstick so she could die slowly and with no one noticing until she dropped dead days later. Nobody knew what had happened, and it took the coroner a long time to figure it out.

Ethan sat straight in the chair, staring defiantly down at me. He visibly sighed. "Nobody liked Candace messing around with the dangerous plants. We warned her not to, but nobody could tell her what to do. At sixteen, she already knew what she wanted out of life, and she studied plants. She was so outgoing and lively then one day everything changed, and nobody knew what had happened. She wore baggy clothing, stopped going out with friends, and hardly ate. I was with her one day when she saw someone she didn't want to. She mumbled the name Tom, and I didn't understand what was going on, until I met Julia and she told me about a man named Tom and what he did to her sister. Memories came back, and that's when I realized it was the same Tom. I found his Body Count book when I snuck into his apartment a couple of days before his death. That's when I saw Candace on the first page and knew his death had to be brutal."

"Did Tom wake up?"

He nodded. "Yeah, Julia was busy with something in the kitchen, and he woke up when I entered his room. I shoved the lipstick into his mouth while telling him how he killed my sister and every woman in that book because of what he did. He hurt so many, and when I found the picture of Pam there and how he wanted to change for her, I hated her even more. I know it wasn't her fault, but still, it took the guy twelve years to sort his shit out, and I know for a fact he didn't put pictures in the book of all the women he fucked."

"What do you mean?"

"All those videos he made of the women. There are hundreds of recordings. Hundreds. Check the tapes. There aren't hundreds of photos in his book."

I nodded, making a note. Our violent crimes unit had taken over the evidence and would check everything. James made a note, too.

I glanced at Ethan, and he had an unwavering death stare. He was going to jail for a long time for premeditated murder, and framing his wife for it, and attempted murder of his wife. Ethan was cunning, devious, and malicious. He'd get along with a lot of men while he was away.

The interview ended soon after that, and we wrote up our reports now that the case was closed on our end.

Chapter Forty-Two

DANA

I WATCHED my brother talk about the case and how messed up Ethan truly was. My face twisted in disgust as I tried understanding how a husband who had loved his wife could be so cold and calculating. James had everything I wanted in a partner; it would devastate me if he had to try do something similar. Ethan was pure evil.

Thank goodness Pamela was managing just fine without Ethan. Her mom cut her holiday short to spend some time with her and the kids. Ethan had various policies that would be paying out, and Pam ensured me that she and the kids were well taken care of. She had also sworn off dating for a while; I didn't blame her.

"Their trials will start next month," Donnie continued. "They're all getting the maximum, especially now that the violent crimes unit have taken over."

"I'm just glad it's over now," I said, squeezing James's hand. He glanced at me and winked.

"Promise me you won't go behind my back again," he said, squeezing my hand back.

"Promise."

"Actually, don't investigate," Donnie interjected. "Come and tell us what's happening otherwise next time I'll arrest you."

"No, you won't." I challenged, narrowing my eyes at him.

"Try me, sister, I will."

"Okay," Mom said, entering the living room. "That's enough, lunch is ready. No more talk about cases and terrible husbands. I want a nice family lunch where we talk about your father and him falling."

Our father had fallen off the ladder earlier this week. His left-hand side was badly bruised, but otherwise he was fine.

Donnie groaned as he stood and stretched his back.

"You sound almost as bad as dad. Don't tell me you're also getting old?" I joked with Donnie.

"You wish," Donnie said. "Dad might be seventy-five but he's still strong. Come, I'm hungry."

"Wait," James said, stopping me from standing.

"What's wrong?" I asked, nestling into his side on the couch.

"Seriously though, I don't want to control everything you do but you need to tell me when you're working a case that might interfere with our active investigation."

I knew this was coming and understood why he raised it now. He felt disrespected as my husband but also it could've ruined their case. Guilt chose that moment to hit me in the face.

"I promise," I said, kissing him chastely. "If anything had gone wrong, I would've come to you sooner."

"I know, but the point is to come to me from the beginning. We could've helped Pam from the beginning. We could've sent her for tests; we could've avoided her almost getting killed. Instead, you told her to run. It was all unnecessary trauma she went through."

"No, I didn't tell her to run. She chose to run. I told her I wanted to call you and Donnie. She begged me not to."

"Okay, I hear you. But are we in agreement?"

"Yes, I promise. No going behind your back. Ever. No matter what someone asks of me."

"Good," he said, standing and pulling me up with him. "Let's eat. Then when we get home, I have a surprise for you."

———

"A CAT?" I said, frowning at this tiny fur ball in a crate.

"Kitten. She's a kitten and we're her mom and dad."

I shuddered at the thought. "You want us to be fur-parents to a scratch-my-eyes-out kitten?"

"Yes, all we have to do is teach her how to use the litter box, feed her, and she'll keep herself entertained," James said, picking up the bundle of joy.

"It's because we don't have children, hey?"

He chuckled. "We agreed we didn't want. And yes, this little thing will give us joy that only an animal can bring. You'll see, you'll enjoy her."

"She is cute," I said, taking her out of his hands and she started purring. "Aah," I said, immediately falling in love with her. "What should we call her?"

"How about Luna?"

"Hm, I like that." I said as Luna licked my fingers. "This was a lovely surprise Mr. Michaels," I said, leaning in to kiss him. "Smooth husband, smooth move."

He laughed. "Let's set everything up for her here."

We walked towards the living room area, sat on the ground, and we got started on Luna's new home with us.

Also by N Gray writing as Natalie Michaels

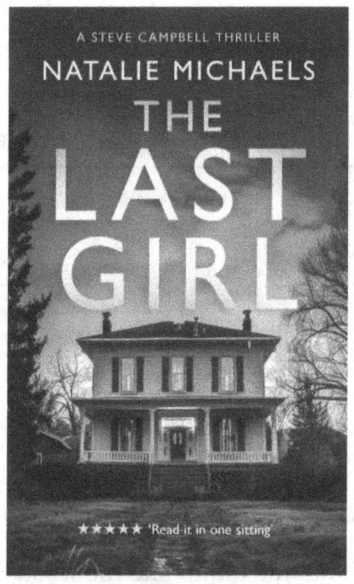

vinci-books.com/lastgirl

Some monsters don't hide—they hunt.

When two women vanish in Ketchum, Detective Steve Campbell uncovers a chilling link to a predator who's been hunting for years. As the clock runs out, he must face the darkest corners of Haskins' lair to save the last girl.

Turn the page for a free preview…

The Last Girl: Chapter One

THE CABIN

Jacob
1987

THE QUIET EVENING pierced my ears. Carefully, I climbed out of the water and onto the wooden deck without making a sound. I exhaled silently as I monitored the couple fast asleep in the boat. Tiptoeing on the wooden deck, I was careful not to stand on a creaking plank and when I reached the door, Katie stirred in the boat, mumbling someone's name. I opened the door, testing to ensure it didn't moan the wider I opened it, and slipped out.

I traversed the dark path to the house and entered. Leaving the lights off, I navigated my way around the living room, kitchen, until finally upstairs. I entered the main bedroom and found his suitcase again. Flipping through his wallet, I found what I was looking for and headed back down to the kitchen. Their food remained on the counter, waiting for them to enjoy, and I opened the pantry door.

Once done, I slipped out the front door and found a place hidden in shadows where I could see most of the house and waited. I heard cars driving on the ID-75 entering and exiting Ketchum and was grateful they were a distance away and wouldn't see me or my vehicle from the road.

It was ten at night by the time Katie and her friend staggered up the path, switching on lights as they entered the house and headed for the kitchen. Katie warmed their dinner while her friend sat at the table, waiting for her to serve him.

The itch at the back of my neck started up again, but I didn't scratch. I just rubbed the offending area and waited.

Katie dished food onto their plates and sat beside him. My body heated as I watched him eat. All was fine for a few seconds and then... he grabbed his throat. His eyes widened in horror. Red blotches formed on his face and neck. His face started swelling, along with one side of his neck. He pushed away from the table, stood up, then doubled over as if trying to expel whatever was lodged in his throat.

Katie was there to slap him on his back, but nothing helped.

Nothing would help him.

The man pointed to the stairs and then to his neck. Katie nodded and frantically ran upstairs.

Moments later, she returned, shaking her head. "There's nothing there," she cried.

Shock flashed in his eyes. He collapsed onto his knees, then fell on his chest and face, unmoving.

Katie dashed around, looking for something, but there was nothing that could help him. She fell to her knees and moved him onto his back so she could proceed with CPR, but his throat had already closed, shutting off all his air supply.

From where I stood, his face and neck had swollen to the point where his cheeks were red, round and puffy, and his eyes had bulged. While his fat lips had started turning purple.

After about ten minutes, Katie sat back on her haunches, crying into her hands.

I dropped the epinephrine injection on the ground and crushed it with my boot heel. Pushing through the branches, I approached the cabin with purpose and entered through the front door.

Katie flinched when she saw me and stood up. "Jacob, what are you doing here?" she asked, glancing nervously at me and then at her friend on the floor.

"I thought you might need some help," I said mysteriously and crossed the threshold. My clothing was still damp, and I left wet marks everywhere I stepped.

Katie backed up, glancing at me and the body. "We need to call for help," she stammered, "could you—"

"No," I yelled, shutting her up. "No more, Katie," I snapped. "You've been playing me for years. No more." I pulled the box out of my pocket and placed it gently on the counter. "I've had this for a while, waiting for the right moment to give it to you. To ask for your hand in marriage. Ever since that day in the barn, I've loved you more than anything else. I would've given you the world, anything, and everything you ever wanted. But," I paused for effect and stared into her sad, blue eyes, "you've made it perfectly clear where I stand with you."

The Last Girl: Chapter Two

THE SECOND WEEK IN DECEMBER

Michelle

2001

JESSICA COMBED her long blond hair and tied it in a low ponytail. She fixed her black top; the one I had bought her for her birthday with the famous Rolling Stones tongue. Then she fastened her belt and pulled on her coat. Grabbing her makeup bag, she applied eyeshadow, mascara that made her green eyes brighter, and lipstick sparingly, transforming her youthful face into a more mature look.

We had become best friends since first grade in the Ernest Hemingway School in Ketchum. Since then, we did nothing without the other. Once a month, we visited Mike, our good friend, and went to O'Brian's Pub for a few beers and a couple of games.

"How do I look?" she asked, twirling.

"Like you're twenty-two," I said, grinning. I pulled on my coat and huddled into it. "How about me?"

"Perfect," she said.

I wiped some makeup out of the corner of my eye and smiled. My eyes had thick eyeliner, highlighting my big brown eyes, and I tied my black hair in a low ponytail. I had a fair complexion and with my hair being naturally black; I looked like a porcelain doll. But I was not as beautiful as Jessica.

"Are you two wenches finished?" Mike yelled outside the bathroom. "I'm hungry, and there's a game with my name on."

"Yeah, yeah, we're done," I said, opening the door.

Mike stood in the doorjamb, blocking my way. He wore his signature black outfit; black army boots, black cargo pants, and a long sleeve black vest with a black jacket over. With his brown hair shaved close to his head, he reminded me of someone who should be in the army and not out drinking.

I waved the air in front of my nose. "You smell like weed again."

"I know. You want some?"

"No, thanks."

"Come," Jessica said, pushing past Mike, "there are men who need to buy us drinks."

"You're such a skank," Mike said, chuckling, his smile reaching his light brown eyes. If it wasn't for the gothic clothing he wore, I thought he was handsome.

"You're just jealous you can't get free drinks." She cooed.

"Whatever, now come," Mike said, jogging down the stairs. "Bye mom," he yelled into the lounge. His mom waved and continued watching her fantasy series.

We climbed into Mike's blue van, his Passion Wagon, and drove the short distance to O'Brian's Pub. It was a quaint little drinking hole where a lot of the residents frequented. The place smelled like stale ale. The bar counter was sticky from years of spillage, and the beer flowed all night long.

Mike parked the van in the only available parking spot, which was right at the back underneath the one lamppost that didn't work. We traversed the recently cleared path as snow continued falling around us.

I entered the pub first, and the heat smacked me in the face. Shivering from the sudden change in temperature, I headed for the bar and stood between two men talking about their workday.

"Oh, I'm sorry. Am I bothering you?" I asked, fluttering my eyelashes.

"No, sweetheart," the man on my right said. "But I would love to buy you a drink?"

"A beer will do," I said, smiling sweetly.

"Hey Nancy," said the same man, "get my lady friend here a beer."

"Make that two, please, kind sir," Jessica said behind me.

"Make it two," he said with a wicked grin. "And who might you be?"

"Jessica," she said, holding out her hand for him to shake.

Nancy gave us our beers.

The man stood to retrieve his wallet from his back pocket, paid, and sat down again. Jessica and I stood on either side of him and kissed him on the cheek.

"Thank you," we said together and disappeared into the crowd near the back, where Mike was already playing a game of pool.

We laughed and joked around. We tampered with

Mike's cue stick every time he tried to take a shot, sipped from his friends' drinks, and enjoyed our evening.

I loved coming here, as did Jessica. We were together, we always had fun, and we never had to pay for anything.

"I feel like a shot," Jessica said, swaying slightly.

"You've had enough," I said, slipping my arm through hers. "How about we ask Nancy for something to eat and two glasses of water?"

"Nah, I want a shot." Jessica unhooked her arm from mine and made a beeline toward the bar. She bumped into a man wearing a blue jacket sitting at the bar and started talking to him. She laughed at whatever he said and sat beside him. They seemed to enjoy each other's company and now and then, Jessica would touch his arm or laugh at whatever he said. Then she thumbed over her shoulder at me. But the man didn't turn around.

Mike cut in front of me, blocking my view. "Move," I moaned and pushed past him. When I could see Jessica again, she downed a shot with the man and then he stood up from his stool. He pointed at the door, and Jessica nodded.

"What are you doing?" I mumbled to myself.

"Where are you going?" Mike asked.

"To stop Jessica from making a big mistake."

"She's a big girl. She can take care of herself."

"She's only nineteen, Mike," I grumbled. "We need to look out for each other."

Mike raised his hands in mock surrender. "Fine, but if you aren't here when I'm ready to go, I'll leave your ass here, too."

I rolled my eyes and headed for the door. Jessica and the man had already left by the time I pulled on my coat. I opened the door, and the cold air stole my breath as I braved the chilly night.

A car's engine rumbled to life in the distance, and I turned to look, but couldn't see much. A light came on and I squinted.

"Jessica?" I yelled and headed for the car. "Jessica?" I yelled again, waving my arms so she could see me.

A car door slammed, and a figure headed my way. "Michelle," Jessica said, closing the gap. "I'm going home with my new friend." She wiggled her eyebrows. "I'll see you at Mike's tomorrow," she slurred, hugging me. When she let me go, her now dull green eyes glazed over as she smiled.

"Are you sure you're in condition to go home with anyone?" I asked.

"Relax, I'm fine. Besides, everyone knows him," she said, turning around.

"Who is he?" I asked. There were moments like now when I hated going out with Jessica. She had gone home with guys once or twice before, but I had always met them beforehand. I didn't know who this guy was, and it left me worried.

"It's fine, he's fine, I'm fine," she mumbled. "I'll see you in the morning." She waved over her shoulder as she walked to his car.

"Who is he?" I yelled, but she didn't hear me.

Once Jessica climbed into his car, he turned around, blinding me with his headlights. Once I could see again, all I saw were his taillights in the distance.

I didn't like her going off with some stranger she had only just met and even though he was someone everybody knew, apparently; I didn't know who he was.

Something didn't sit right with me, but I shook off the bad feeling. She was a young adult and could handle herself.

When I went back inside the pub, I had sobered up and asked Mike if we could leave. He handed me the keys and asked me to drive.

Once back at his place, I settled into the bed beside him, and he started snoring; I laid awake with worry.

———

THE NEXT MORNING, when Jessica didn't come home, I asked Mike to take me to the police station. I waited to speak with an officer, filled out forms, and explained what had happened.

When Monday came and went and Jessica still hadn't come home, and I hadn't heard from the detective, I went back to the police station. They reassured me they were investigating and would give me feedback by Wednesday.

Wednesday passed, and the detective called me on Thursday to let me know they had no leads or witnesses. He also informed me that there were many people at O'Brian's Pub and Nancy didn't remember Jessica or me being there, therefore nobody knew who the man was she had gone home with.

When Friday arrived and I still had heard nothing, I asked Mike to go with me to the pub, but because Christmas was next Tuesday, he was taking his mother to visit his aunt in Sun Valley.

I went alone to the pub, but it was empty, with only a few patrons; none of them remembered me and I couldn't recall them either. I came home early and vowed to go the next weekend and the next until I found out who Jessica's kidnapper was.

If he was local, he had to return.

The Last Girl: Chapter Three

TOUGHEN UP

Jacob - 8 years old
1974

MAMA HAD a headache and didn't join us at church today. Papa told me we had to hurry home because he needed to tend to the sheep.

"I need to use the bathroom," I said, shifting uncomfortably in the backseat.

"We'll be home soon," Papa said, slowing the car as we drove through the town. He waved at Kip and Gladys, who worked at the Ketchum post office. I found it strange they were at work since they rarely opened on a Sunday.

I ground my teeth when Papa went over a bump, rocking the car. "Papa, please, can you stop? I need to use the bathroom."

"Toughen up, boy, we're almost home."

Tears welled in my eyes. Pain erupted in my tummy.

"Oh Jesus, fine, I'll stop at the gas station."

As Papa stopped the car, I bolted out, but I didn't make it to the bathroom in time. I stopped a stone's throw away from the door that led to the men's bathroom. The warm urine ran down my leg, in my shoe, and absorbed into the dry sand.

"Oh shucks," Papa said beside me, "it looks like you didn't make it after all. You can be lucky you didn't do that in my car." He chuckled. "I would've beaten you so badly if you messed in my car."

"Jacob wet his pants. Jacob wet his pants," three boys sang as they passed us on their bicycles. They were from my class and I knew they would tease me at school tomorrow again.

My cheeks heated, and I covered my crotch area with my hands. I glanced up at Papa, who still grinned down at me.

"Come, you've already wet yourself. Might as well climb into the car like that." Papa climbed into his car and started the engine. He glanced over his shoulder, staring at me.

Heat rose into my chest, and neck and I fisted my little hands.

"Move it," he yelled.

I stomped toward the car, opened the door, and climbed inside, slamming the door closed. My cold, damp pants stuck to my skin, making me shiver. I folded my arms across my chest, and I didn't want to look at him.

"You will become a man one day and you need to stand up for yourself," Papa said, glancing at me in his rear-view mirror now and then while he drove. "And one of those things is managing your bladder. You can't go around pissing your pants."

"Yes, Papa," I said, glancing out of the window. Our farm was on the outskirts of Ketchum, a quiet mountain town far from any city, yet close enough that one didn't want to go anywhere. Mountains surrounded our town with crystal clear waterways, hiking, and biking trails, and when it snowed everybody went skiing.

"And you need to stand up to those boys," Papa said. "They're going to bully you."

I didn't want to talk to him anymore, so I continued glancing out of the window, watching the world go by.

We passed the local cemetery where they had buried Ernest Hemingway. Mama had told me a story about the famous author and how he killed himself. They diagnosed him with some disease I couldn't pronounce. His father, sister and brother also killed themselves; I hoped I didn't get what they had.

Papa turned onto the dirt road leading up to our farmhouse and relief washed over me; I could take a nice bath and put on dry clothing. I wrinkled my nose at the smell of my urine-stained pants.

When Papa stopped the car, I climbed out and sprinted up the path toward the house, then stopped when Papa called me.

"Hurry, boy, you have chores to do."

"Yes, Papa," I said, climbing up the veranda stairs. When Papa was no longer looking at me, I bolted through the open front door, slamming it behind me. Then ran up the stairs to my bedroom and peeled the wet clothing from my body, throwing them in the laundry basket.

Hushed voices sounded outside my bedroom door, and then water started running in the bath.

There was a soft knock on my door. "Jacob," Mama said, slowly opening the door. "I've run your bath water."

"Thank you," I said, pulling off my damp underwear. "Sorry," I said, averting my eyes.

"It's ok, my son. Perhaps you should've gone before you left church."

"I wanted to, but Papa said to hurry."

She stared down at me with an expression I didn't understand. "Try harder next time because it will be difficult to clean your shoes." She picked up my soiled clothing and shoes and exited. "Hurry and bathe, your father needs you outside."

"Mama?"

She stopped and glanced over her shoulder. "What is it?"

"Why is Papa so hard on me?" I asked, my bottom lip trembling slightly.

Mama opened her mouth to say something but closed her mouth instead.

"Moira!" Papa yelled from downstairs. "Where's my boots?"

"In the closet near the front door."

"Now why did you move it there."

Mama rolled her eyes. "You left them there, Bill," she yelled.

"Don't talk back to me like that, woman."

"Yes, dear," she said, then turned back to me. "Honey," she started, then stopped as if there was something she wanted to say. "Never mind. Now hurry and be a good boy and go do your chores like Papa wants."

"Ok," I said and ran into the bathroom, slamming the door shut. I washed as quickly as possible, dried, and put on my work clothing. I didn't want Papa yelling at me again today.

The chore Papa had left for me to do was what I hated doing the most; to clean the chicken coop. But once that was done, I sat under my favorite oak tree that stood on a small hill a distance away from the farmhouse.

Papa's sheep roamed freely, grazing everything they could find.

I sat by the tree and watched the sunset. It was the first time this afternoon that I felt better after messing my pants. I felt safer and calmer out here.

Something moved out of the corner of my eye and I glanced in that direction. A wild hare sat staring at me. Slowly, I stood up and approached. The hare waited. I pounced. I caught the hare by its tail with my left hand and dug my fingernails into its body with my right hand.

I gritted my teeth as I applied more pressure. The hare made strange growling hissing sounds as it tried to get away. And I squeezed harder until bones broke.

Once I had secured the hare in my hands, I stood up. With one hand gripping it, I pulled the string out of my pocket and wrapped it around its neck. I tied the knot, ensuring the string was tight, and tied the other end of the string around a tree branch.

I watched the hare suffer while it died. There was something primitive yet satisfying about what I had done. I didn't understand it, only that I enjoyed it and wanted to do it again.

Grab your copy...
vinci-books.com/lastgirl

About the Author

N. Gray is a USA Today Bestselling Author who lives in Cape Town, South Africa, with her daughter and adopted cat named Miss Beans. During the day, she's an analyst and provider profiler for a medical insurance company. At night, she types on her curved keyboard, creating fictional characters some may love and others you may want to kill yourself.

She writes in four genres: urban fantasy, thriller, horror, and paranormal romance.

She now writes under Natalie Michaels for her new thrillers and SD Syns for her new horrors.